The

Mystery of

Mound Key

The Mystery of Mound Key

ROBERT F. BURGESS

illustrated by Vic Donahue

AN AUTHORS GUILD BACKINPRINT.COM EDITION

AN AUTHORS GUILD BACKINPRINT.COM EDITION

Published by iUniverse.com, Inc.

For information address:
iUniverse.com, Inc.
620 North 48th Street, Suite 201
Lincoln, NE 68504-3467
www.iuniverse.com

Originally published by World Publishing

ISBN: 0-595-00348-6

Printed in the United States of America

To Mother and Dad
for sharing with me
the treasure of those
first outdoor adventures;
to Miss Betty and Mr. Edgar
for their many, many kindnesses;
and to Julie
for her courage and faith
above and beyond the calling
of a writer's wife
this book is most humbly dedicated

Contents

CONTENTS

The

Mystery of

Mound Key

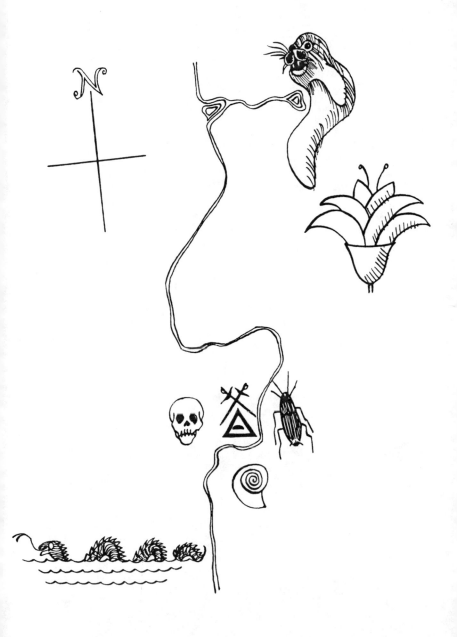

The Old Brass Telescope

S HANDY M CS HANE vaulted the back fence and ran
quickly across a stretch of sand and palmettos to a thick
clump of ti-ti. He pushed his way through the bushes until
he stood behind a thin row of bamboo that screened Jib
Woods's yard from the drifting sand and swampland beyond. Once inside the swale, he could not be seen from
either side. Cupping his hands and putting them to his
mouth, he whistled like a whippoorwill three times.

In a moment Jib's round face appeared at an upstairs
window. Seconds later he came out the back door and ran
to the thicket.

"Shandy?"

"Here."

The boy glanced over his shoulder, then slid through the
prickly bamboo until he stood at his friend's side.

"What's up?"

"I can't tell you here. C'mon."

They pushed their way out of the ti-ti and ran through the palmettos until they reached a sandy path that led them up and across some steep sand dunes. Below them was a long, white beach. Beyond it stretched the Gulf of Mexico, as quiet and blue as the sky. Jib was puffing like a steam engine.

"What're we running for?" he gasped. "Somebody chasing us?"

"No, not yet," said Shandy.

"Well, you're going like you got a bee inside of you."

"I have," said Shandy. "A big bee." But he slowed to a brisk walk so his chubby friend could catch up.

"Mr. Scanlon's back in town," he said quietly.

"Huh?" Jib missed a step.

"That's not all," Shandy went on. "He bought Uncle Martin's sea chest from Aunt Tilou and I'll bet you anything he's looking for the scope."

Jib's eyes widened. "Gee whiz, then we haven't any time to lose!"

Shandy nodded and tapped something he had concealed under his shirt. "That's why I brought it along. If anybody can help us, Catfish can."

And without another word the two boys hurried over the crest of a white dune, and in a flurry of sand they half-ran, half-slid down the other side to Phillips Inlet and a spotlessly clean houseboat moored at the shore.

"Hey—!" snorted Catfish Jackson, jerking back from a cast net he was repairing on the foredeck. Then he grinned.

"Golly, for a second there I thought a whole herd of swamp hogs was stampeding over the dunes. Shake off your sand and come aboard."

The boys scampered across the gangplank and Catfish shuffled aft to meet them. He was barefoot as usual, and his patched khakis were rolled up just short of his knees. He wore a dinky red stocking cap cocked to one side and pulled low on his forehead.

"What's all the rush about?" he asked, hanging up his net and running a hand through his stubbly white beard.

"Just wait!" Jib gasped. "Wait till you see what Shandy and me found in the old sea chest—the one we haven't got any more," he added as a sad afterthought.

Catfish's eyebrows danced. "Ahhh—a real treasure this time, I'll bet."

"How'd you know?" exclaimed Jib, dumfounded.

Catfish winked. "Well, out with it, lads. Don't keep ol' Catfish waiting."

"Not here," said Shandy, clutching the mysterious bundle under his shirt. "Somebody might see us."

"Well, I guess if it's that secret a treasure," said Catfish, "we better go in the cabin to look at it. Besides," he added, "I think there might be some ham and eggs in the galley waiting to be fried. Y'all can stow the treasure long enough to eat some breakfast, can't you?"

"Yes sir! Even if it is my third breakfast," Jib spoke up quickly.

Shandy groaned. "Now you've ruined it," he said.

"Ruined what?" asked the pudgy boy innocently.

Shandy wasn't sure. "I don't know," he said. "But whatever it was, it isn't there any more." He shook his head. "And we came on business."

"Now, now," said Catfish. "You gotta remember a ten-year-old boy has a mighty big appetite, Shandy."

"Right," agreed Jib, promptly squaring his shoulders. "And when I get to be twelve like Shandy, I expect it'll be even a bigger one."

The sea captain's blue eyes twinkled. "Yes sir," he said, "I reckon it will at that." He opened the door and led the way into the cabin.

The inside of Catfish Jackson's cabin was a sight to see. It looked something like a museum. All along the front bulkhead that separated the cabin from the tiny wheelhouse there were rows and rows of fishing lures of all colors hooked into pieces of cork from old life jackets. Mounted above them was a five-foot bill from a sawfish and along all its edges were big sharp teeth. On the port side over the portholes were the white jawbones of a tiger shark with all its teeth. On the opposite side over the portholes were two harpoons and a five-pronged gig lying on brass brackets. All over the upper bulkhead, except where there was a skylight, were fishing rods, big ones and small ones, the reels turned up and hooked to the cabin beams. Over the door was a small map of the United States. There were four bunks forward. Down the middle of the cabin, bolted to the deck, was a long table with folding chairs that could be put under the bunks when more room was needed. The galley was squeezed between the bunks and storage closets.

Two brass lanterns hung from the skylight grille. Shandy thought the cabin had the coziest look of any room he'd ever seen.

Catfish Jackson produced a king-sized frying pan, lit his two-burner cookstove, and put it on to heat. The boys sat down at the table. "You can start telling me about this find of yours whenever you're a-mind to," said Catfish over his shoulder as he brought a bowl of eggs and a thick slab of country-cured bacon out of his miniature icebox under the stove.

"Well," Shandy began, "you remember me telling you how Uncle Martin always collected things?"

"You mean the things he'd bring home from some of his salvage trips?"

"That's right," said Shandy. "He was always saving stuff from old shipwrecks. Most of it got put in his old sea chest in the attic."

"That's right," remembered Catfish, breaking the eggs and dropping them between the sizzling pieces of bacon in the frying pan. "That was the same chest where you and Jib found that Japanese diving helmet."

Jib smothered a giggle. "Shandy doesn't talk about that any more," he said.

Shandy frowned at his friend who had turned to sniff the appetizing hickory-smoke aroma drifting from the pan of bacon and eggs.

"I couldn't help getting my head caught in it," he said. "Even if it was dented we still could have made a neat space helmet out of it."

"I take it your Aunt Tilou didn't think much of the idea," said Catfish.

"She had to take him to the doctor to get it off," said Jib.

"Anyway," went on Shandy, anxious to forget the matter, "that was the chest. After Uncle Martin died, one of the men from the salvage company brought out a few other things he had left in the office. Aunt Tilou put them all in the chest and said she wished she knew of a junkman who would take it away. But out here on the beach where we live, there aren't any junkmen, so—"

"It was after she said that that Shandy thought we'd better do some salvaging of our own," interrupted Jib. "And just in time, too, because now Mr. Scanlon has come clear up from Panama City to get the sea chest, and it's not for any old Japanese helmet!"

"I see," said Catfish, using a pancake flipper to put the eggs and bacon on their plates. "And what'd you find?"

"Well," said Shandy, "at first we thought it was an old piece of pipe. It was all green and covered with chalky stuff that would come off on your hands. But in one place we saw where somebody had cleaned that off, right down to the metal. The metal was yellow and there was a picture scratched in it."

Catfish Jackson turned around with the pancake flipper poised in mid-air. He frowned. "A picture?" he said.

Shandy nodded. "We cleaned it up," he said, "and there wasn't just one picture, but a lot of them. In fact," he added, "it's some kind of a map!"

"Whoa, now," said Catfish, wiping his hands on a towel. "Let's see this find of yours."

Shandy reached inside his shirt and withdrew the bundle. Slowly he unrolled it from a piece of old sailcloth, enjoying every minute of it like a magician pulling a rabbit out of a hat. Finally it was unwrapped and he handed it to the captain.

"Well, I'll be—" Catfish said, turning it over slowly in his hands. "It's an old brass spyglass—or what was one. Did you boys clean it up like this?"

"It took a lot of steel wool and polishing," said Jib proudly, "but we finally got it shiny."

"What do the pictures mean?" Shandy asked eagerly.

Catfish furrowed his brow. "Can't say as I know. It's a map all right—you can tell by this crude compass rose." He put his finger on two crossed lines, one with the letter *N* above it. The pictures went on down the barrel of the telescope. "Some of them look like fish. Or sea monsters, maybe. Leastways I've never seen the likes of them before."

"Look at that picture near the triangle," said Shandy, pointing. "It's a cross."

Catfish held the telescope away from him and squinted at it. "It sure is a cross," he said. "It's two crossed swords!"

Shandy glanced sharply at Jib. "Then it *is* a pirate's treasure map—just what we guessed!"

"And Mr. Scanlon is after it to get to the treasure first!" Jib said.

"Now, don't be too sure," cautioned Catfish, drawing out a chair and sitting down to ponder the boys' find. "The scope looks old all right. Maybe a couple of hundred years or more. But even then the pictures could be just some seaman's doodling. They might not mean anything."

"But they've got to mean something," said Shandy. "What do you think, Jib?"

"I think our eggs have gotten cold," said Jib Woods hungrily.

"Oh, no," groaned Shandy.

While the boys ate their ham and eggs, Catfish studied the scope.

"I reckon those pictures are really symbols," he said, "pictures that have a meaning, but maybe not the kind of meaning you first think of when you see the picture. Look here a minute." He took the scope and pointed to the crossed lines with the *N* above the middle line. "This is a compass rose, just like on a real compass. It tells us that this other wavy line runs almost true north and south. Now, that line could be a river or a coastline. And if it's a coast-line there's nothing written that says whether it's an east or a west coast. But look down here," said Catfish, turning the scope so they could see the horizontal peaked lines with a picture of a snake crossing them. "This tells us right away which coast it is. Old-time sailors thought the sea was full of serpents and monsters. Whoever made this map put a sea serpent where the sea was—so that makes this wavy line a west coast, and the other pictures are for things inland."

"Gosh," said Jib, "how'd you ever figure that out?"

Catfish chuckled. "That part isn't hard, Jib. Compass roses are on all the maps we have today and it's just com- mon sense that a sea serpent shown swimming in water isn't likely to be on land anywhere." He pointed to one of the other pictures. "What's that look like to you?"

"The top of a palm tree," said Jib.

"That's close. But look again."

"Is it a flower?" asked Shandy.

"Sure it is," said Catfish. "And why would a pirate draw a picture of a flower unless it meant something? In this picture language of his he's saying this west coast isn't the west coast of South America or the Dry Tortugas or any other place—it's the 'Land of Flowers.' In Spanish the word is *Florida*."

"Boy-o-boy!" exclaimed Jib.

"Gosh, maybe it isn't going to be so hard to unpuzzle after all," said Shandy.

Catfish spread his hands. "I wouldn't count on that," he said. "The best I can figure, looking at these lines, is that they are supposed to be rivers or creeks. The circles in front of them must be islands. As for the rest of the pictures . . ." he shrugged.

Shandy looked closely at the telescope. At the beginning of one of the rivers was a picture of another sea monster, one with a face like a frog and a tail like a beaver. Farther down the map was a triangle with a black half moon inside it. The pictures around the triangle were two crossed swords, something that looked like a beetle, a skull, and a coiled line.

"Let's try to figure out what that half moon in the triangle means," said Catfish. "The only half moons I've ever seen have been in almanacs. It means half moon under, or something like that," he guessed.

"That can't be right," said Jib. "Anybody knows pirates always buried their treasure in the dark of the moon. It looks like a slice of watermelon to me."

"Well, they mark mud flats and marshes on geodetic maps. Maybe a pirate could have put his favorite watermelon patch on this one," said Catfish.

The boys looked at him to see if he was kidding, but his face was blank.

Finally, after several more ideas had been mentioned, they gave up and went on to the other pictures.

Catfish pointed to the bug and said it might be a scarab.

"What's a scarab?" they asked.

"You must have read about scarabs," explained Catfish. "Sometimes the ancient Egyptians used to bury them with their dead for good luck."

Jib said it looked like a plain old roach to him but Catfish stuck to his idea that it was a good-luck sign. "The crossed swords must mean that if there's a treasure, it's buried there," he said. "*X* always marks the spot."

"And pirates always buried some of the crew with the treasure," put in Jib, caught up in the excitement of breaking the mysterious picture code. "Dead men tell no tales—that's what the skull means."

"Now you're getting the idea," said Catfish enthusiastically.

But the last picture puzzled them the most. Finally Shandy said, "It looks like a coiled rope . . . or a snake . . . or a snail . . . or a—"

Catfish snapped his fingers. "Wait a minute—a snail! A snail shell, that's what it is! There's shell piles all over the state but most of them are on the coast. And that's the triangle—a pyramid of shells! Since it's drawn in a bay, it must be a shell island!"

"But who piled them up like that?" asked Jib.

"The Indians did. They ate clams, snails, conchs— every kind of shellfish they could find. Afterward the shells were always thrown on the same pile. In the hundred years or so before the pirates showed up they were already sizable piles, maybe as high as a house. By and by the tribes moved on and the only signs they left of their camps were heaps of shells. They're natural landmarks."

"Then if that's right," said Jib, "we got to look for a shell island just below a chunk of coast that sticks out like a Georgia ham."

"Right," said Catfish, "and if we don't figure out what that bump in the coast is we might just as well forget about going. There's shell islands all along the Gulf."

For a moment the boys were speechless.

"Going! You mean we could go after it on the *Albatross?*" asked Shandy, hardly daring to believe his ears.

"Why not? Your summer vacation's just started and this old boat's been drydocked long enough as it is."

"Gosh," gasped Jib, "if we only *could!*"

"We could if your folks'd be agreeable," said Catfish.

Shandy groaned. "Aunt Tilou would never let me go treasure hunting," he said gloomily. "She doesn't know anything about the telescope."

"Maybe if I talked to her it'd help," Catfish suggested. "Since we aren't *sure* it's a pirate's map, I see no need to bring it up. Besides, we're in no hurry and a trip like that would be a fine chance for you to see something of Florida. A sea trip's an education in itself."

The more Shandy thought about it, the more he could see Aunt Tilou looking at it from that point of view. "Anything that's got education to it sure would appeal to Aunt Tilou," he said.

"My folks are planning a trip to Alabama," said Jib. "I'm supposed to go too but I'd run away just to go with you and Shandy on the *Albatross*."

Catfish chuckled good-naturedly. "I don't think you have to do anything that serious, Jib. If we decide to go I'll talk to your folks and see what they think about it." Catfish got up and lit the two lanterns over the table.

"The first thing we got to do," he said, "is find out where we're going." He opened a narrow bulkhead closet and brought out several rolls of paper.

"These are geodetic maps," he said, putting them on the table.

"What's a geo— geodetic map?" asked Jib.

"It's a chart sailors use for finding their way around the sea," Catfish explained, unrolling one of the maps. "Each one shows an enlarged part of the coastline with things like landmarks, shipping lanes, compass bearings, channels and the like."

"What are those numbers in the water?" asked Shandy.

"They tell you how deep the water is so you won't run your boat aground."

"Gee, then it's kind of like a road map, but for the sea," said Shandy.

"That's it exactly. Now let's see what we can figure out."

But hours later they were still as baffled as when they started. None of the maps looked exactly like the one on the telescope.

"That pirate must not have been too smart if he didn't know enough to put better directions on his map," said Jib in disgust.

Shandy agreed. Catfish Jackson tilted his chair back and slid his feet out straight in front of him. He yawned and looked as if he were going to sleep. But instead he was squinting at the cabin roof. All of a sudden he stared at something. He was looking at the small map of the United States tacked just over the door.

Kar-rack! His chair legs hit the deck. "Scuttle my locker!" he roared. "Le'me see that Tampa map again!"

The boys went through the pile of charts and pulled it out. Catfish squinted at it. "What nincompoops we are!" he shouted. "Look yonder at the United States map. What's that bump on the west coast of Florida if it's not where Tampa Bay makes a big peninsula? Why, it's plain as the nose on your face! That's what we been looking for!" He waved the telescope excitedly. "Reason we couldn't find it on the charts was because they only show enlarged parts of the coast. We were looking for something smaller. But that's it, there's rivers above and below it and shell islands aplenty, just like the scope shows. Now we can get started for that treasure!"

Catfish Pays a Visit

THE NEXT MORNING Shandy couldn't believe his eyes when he came downstairs. Catfish Jackson was sitting in the sunroom sipping a cup of tea and talking with Aunt Tilou. What struck Shandy was that it was the first time he'd ever seen Catfish really dressed up. He had on a white suit with a polka-dot tie that had a stickpin in it. His shoes were so clean that Shandy knew he must have carried them all the way from Phillips Inlet to keep them that way. Shandy was tiptoeing toward the kitchen when his aunt called him.

"Shandy, come here a minute. Mr. Jackson has come to visit."

Shandy went as far as the doorway. He nodded and spoke to Catfish, then looked at his aunt.

"Come in and sit down," she said, beckoning him toward a chair.

He sat down but he felt ill at ease. Mostly what made

26

him uncomfortable was the change that had come over Catfish. The captain and Aunt Tilou went on talking. Catfish didn't once forget himself and say "well scuttle something" or take out his corncob pipe and suck on it. He just sat there straight and sipped tea out of a cup so tiny that he couldn't begin to get his finger through the handle— just as if he'd done it every morning of his life.

Sandy listened while they talked about the weather a bit and then about the pitiful state of the world. Then they switched to Aunt Tilou's favorite subject: kinfolk. Shandy wished they'd get on with the important part of their talk. The longer he waited, the more uncomfortable he got. First he got an itch on his leg and just as he was reaching for it, it jumped down to his foot. He kicked himself in the ankle and had to grit his teeth. Then the side of his neck began to itch. From there it went to his ear where he gave it a good cuff. But that started it in the middle of his back. He was reaching for it with both arms when Aunt Tilou turned and leveled her eyes on him.

"*Really*, Mr. Jackson, any boy who squirms and fidgets so much as this one does is no fit companion for a sea trip," she said pointedly.

Shandy sat up straight and tried not to act as if he knew what she was talking about.

"Mr. Jackson has been telling me that you and Jib Woods would like to take a trip on his boat," continued Aunt Tilou.

"Yes'm," said Shandy.

"I've already explained it, Shandy, and your aunt's given half her permission for you to go."

"Really, Aunt Tilou?" Shandy jumped up and threw his arms around her neck.

"Here now, you'll get my glasses all steamed," she said, flustered. "Yes, I said you might go on one condition—that you wouldn't forget to write me from time to time."

"Why, Auntie, I'd write you every single chance I got," promised Shandy.

Aunt Tilou smiled and put her arm around him. "Since your uncle isn't here to take you on trips like this, Shandy, I think it's very kind of Mr. Jackson to ask you to go."

"Then that settles it," grinned Catfish, getting up. After politely thanking Aunt Tilou for the tea, he added, "I've got some other calls to make, then we'll get together, Shandy, and plan out the equipment we'll take."

"Swell," said Shandy. He walked Catfish to the door. When he was sure his aunt wouldn't hear, he whispered, "Hope you have the same luck at Jib's house."

Catfish winked, then waved and went off down the street.

Shandy hurried up to his room where he started getting out things he would need for the trip. In an hour he had a few clothes and a large pile of other things ready to stuff into a blue duffel bag. He was just preparing to pack when he heard Jib's whistle. Dropping everything, he hurried downstairs and out the door.

"It's all set!" Jib yelled gleefully. "Catfish fixed it so I can go!"

The two boys congratulated each other until they were blue in the face, then broke into fits of happy laughter.

"Good ol' Catfish," gasped Shandy. "I knew he wouldn't let us down."

"And didn't he look swell though, and talk nice?"

"Better'n anyone I ever saw. I'd bet that if Catfish was to run for President of the United States he'd get it, hands down."

"Gee," said Jib, "there wouldn't be anybody foolish enough to take that bet."

"I wonder when we'll go," said Shandy.

"Let's go down to the *Albatross* and ask him right now."

They started to run out of the yard, and ran head on into a tall, thin man who was just coming through the gate.

"Hello boys," he said coolly.

Shandy swallowed hard and said, "H-hello, Mr. Scanlon." As far back as Shandy could remember, his Uncle Martin's partner had always worn a tight-fitting black suit, and he had a way of jerking his outthrust jaw as if his collar were tight too. Now he stood in their way, holding the gate half open while his gray eyes darted from one boy to the other and his jaw jerked nervously. Finally Mr. Scanlon's lips drew back into a tight grin.

"You've grown since I've been in South America," he said, fixing his gaze on Shandy.

"Yes, sir," said Shandy, dropping his gaze.

"Your aunt," he said. "Is she home?"

"Yes sir, I'll call her right away." Relieved at the excuse to get away, Shandy whirled and raced back up onto the porch and called Aunt Tilou.

She hurried out, wiping her hands on her apron and greeting Mr. Scanlon uncertainly. He and Uncle Martin had been partners in the salvage business, but they had never been really friendly. Shandy stepped aside with the idea of slipping by them and getting away. But once again Mr. Scanlon occupied the main avenue of escape and Shandy felt the restraining hand of his Aunt Tilou close on his arm as he tried to squeeze by.

"It's nice seeing you and Shandy again," said Mr. Scanlon, ignoring Jib, who was waiting quietly within hearing by the edge of the porch. "It's hard to believe that it's been six months since Martin died." Mr. Scanlon's jaw jerked twice in rapid succession. "Anyway," he continued, "I wanted to drop by as soon as I got back from South America to tell you how much I enjoyed going over all those old things he collected through the years. Nothing of value, of course . . ."

"I understand," said Aunt Tilou. "Martin was always bringing something home, something he either found or was given. Sakes alive, I imagine he'd be glad to know you have them, you both being in the salvage business and all."

Shandy was beginning not to feel too good.

"The boy, here, was a little upset though," continued Aunt Tilou with a tinge of regret in her voice as she touched his shoulder. "He and his friend took a great liking to his Uncle Martin's chest. You know how boys are," she smiled gently.

Shandy closed his eyes and bit his lower lip. The chest with the dented helmet, the ship's bell, the bits of coral, the rusty marlin spikes, the old pulleys, the cannon balls, the grapeshot, the slave chains, the worm-eaten but carved mahogany railing—all of it was gone. She had sold everything to Mr. Scanlon for five dollars!

"I wouldn't waste my time worrying about it if I were

you," said Mr. Scanlon, dropping his eyes to Shandy as his long white fingers absently crinkled the cellophane wrappings of a row of cigars in his breast pocket. "Any self-respecting junkman wouldn't have looked twice at the things in that chest. I just enjoy having them around as reminders of the hard days when your uncle and I used to do our own diving. Now, when I was your age, I wanted something worth while, something of value." Mr. Scanlon's hand came down from his pocket and doubled into a tight bony fist. "The feel of real coins in my hand. That's what a boy your age should be interested in. Hard cash, son. That's what makes the world go 'round."

"Yes sir," said Shandy quietly.

"However," Mr. Scanlon said, turning again to Aunt Tilou, "there was one item I was certain Martin had, but I didn't find it among the things in the chest. I wondered if it could have been overlooked."

Shandy and Jib looked at each other.

"I can't imagine what that could be," said Aunt Tilou.

"It was an old telescope," said Mr. Scanlon with a tight smile. "Of course it didn't look like one," he said. "Looked more like a length of pipe covered with marine formations. It was very old. Ruined, naturally, by salt water. Still, I rather fancied it. Martin did most of the salvage work on the wreck it came from so he kept it."

Aunt Tilou frowned. "Goodness, I can't say as I recall ever seeing it. As far as I know, everything Martin ever collected was in the chest when you bought it."

"I see," said Mr. Scanlon solemnly, but he wasn't looking at Aunt Tilou any more. He was looking hard at

Shandy. He didn't say much after that, only that if the telescope should turn up he would appreciate her letting him know. Aunt Tilou promised to do so.

After he left she shook her head and said, to no one in particular, "My goodness, can you imagine a grown man that interested in a little old piece of rusty pipe?"

"No'm," mumbled Shandy, and let it go at that.

As soon as Aunt Tilou went back into the house, the two boys hurried to Phillips Inlet and the *Albatross*.

Catfish was sitting on the fantail in his rolled-up khakis and red stocking cap, looking more like his old self again. The boys wasted no time telling him about Mr. Scanlon's interest in the scope. While he listened, Catfish calmly puffed his pipe and squinted out into the sun glare of the inlet.

When they finished he stood up, rapped his corncob smartly against the boat's railing, and turned to face them. His eyes fairly crackled.

"If we're going to do anything about that treasure," he said, "the time is ripe right now."

"Great!" shouted Shandy, jumping to his feet.

"Yes sir!" joined in Jib, bounding up beside him. "What all do we need to take with us?"

"Whatever camping and swimming gear you got."

"We've both got face masks and flippers," said Shandy.

"Bring 'em," said Catfish. "You'll probably want to do some skin diving in the Gulf."

"Should we take our scuba gear?" asked Shandy.

"Glad you reminded me," said Catfish. "I wanted to be sure and borrow that gasoline-operated air compressor from

Bernie's Garage. Then we won't have to worry about an air supply. You boys remember everything you learned about those rigs, don't you?"

"Yes sir. We've been diving for lost fishing lures all spring at the jetties."

"Good. I'll borrow a truck and run the gear into town for a checkup before we leave," said Catfish. "Might be a good idea to pick up several spare air tanks too, in case we need 'em." The captain pulled a scrap of paper out of his pocket and scribbled a note on it. "Rifle cartridges," he said. "Don't want to forget them. We may run into sharks." Then, with a grim look back at the dunes, he added, "the two-legged kind."

Anchors
Aweigh

IT TOOK THEM almost three days to load everything aboard the houseboat. Once they started, it seemed there was no end to the things they thought they might need. There were shovels and lanterns, great coils of rope and pulleys, machetes, bush axes, and camping things. They rigged up spare anchors, cleaned and greased the big winch that sat just ahead of the wheelhouse. Catfish borrowed Ed Statton's truck from the Beach Shopping Center and carried back gasoline in five-gallon cans that they lugged across the dunes and emptied in the *Albatross'* fuel tanks. When these were filled, there were five-gallon plastic jugs of drinking water to be carried aboard and carefully stowed. After that came boxes of food, enough to feed an army. And finally, when it was all packed away, the *Albatross* squatted so low in the water that she looked like a pelican that had just eaten its fill of cigar minnows. The last thing

34

that went aboard was Catfish's skiff. They hauled it out of water and lashed it, bottom side up, ahead of the winch on the foredeck.

Saying the good-bys was the worst part of all. Aunt Tilou said she wouldn't come to the boat because she didn't want to go through it over again. She did it all before Shandy left, hugging and fussing over him and filling his pockets with odds and ends she was sure he would need. Then she cried a little and made him promise to send postcards along the way, and if he got sick, to telephone her. At last Jib came and saved him. With a final wave, they were on their way.

Catfish was sitting on deck smoking his pipe when they showed up. "The tide's right and the barometer's steady," he said cheerfully. "Looks as if we'll have a good day of it. Let's shove off."

The boys untied the fore and aft hawsers mooring the houseboat to shore, then hurried aboard and drew in the gangplank behind them.

In the wheelhouse, Catfish stuck his head out the window to make sure everything was clear. He had switched his stocking cap for a faded blue captain's cap. The radio was on and the boys could hear the garbled weather reports from New Orleans and the chatter between bottom-fishing boats seventy miles out in the Gulf.

Shandy felt the *Albatross* shudder as Catfish started the motor. While it warmed up he took a last look around the bay, knowing that he wouldn't be seeing it again for some time. The water was like glass. Mullet were jumping just off shore, throwing their silver bodies high into the air and hitting again with a loud splash. Deep in the swamp the birds had awakened and their chirping cries were carried across the bay along with the sweet smell of wet moss. It was a perfect morning.

The motor took on a new sound. Water boiled as the stern moved slowly away from shore. Then the motor reversed. The *Albatross* shook again and the blunt-nosed bow swung out and moved forward, biting into the water, the propeller churning the houseboat toward the long-span bridge over the bay.

The boat slipped beneath the steel structure, plowed its way down the channel between the sand flats, and turned into the main outlet to the Gulf of Mexico. Sun danced on the pale blue water like bursts of fire. A flock of sea gulls rose from the beach and sailed overhead, welcoming them to the great expanse of water they were entering.

The tide was full and slack as the white boat nosed through the cross waves at the entrance of the channel. Catfish steered a straight course until the cut was well astern. The water smoothed into gentle swells and the color changed from pale blue to deep indigo. They were past the last bar now and the *Albatross* heeled slightly as the captain turned the wheel and set her on a southeasterly course. At his elbow was a fathometer whirring in its box as its pen charted an outline of the depths beneath them. Catfish reached over and shut it off. They were in deep water now. He stuck his head out of the wheelhouse window and beamed at Shandy and Jib standing on the bow.

"Saint George Island—here we come!" he yelled.

A sea breeze sang through the radio antenna over the

cabin. Sea gulls gathered behind the boat, wheeling, calling, and swooping in flashing white crescents against the cloudless blue sky. Shandy and Jib pulled off their tennis shoes, stowed them in the lee of the skiff, and then went into the wheelhouse.

"Bluefish and cobia been running," said Catfish. "You boys better tackle up and see what you can do about catching us something for dinner."

"Right away, skipper!" Shandy and Jib hurried into the cabin for their fishing gear.

"Let's try the spinning rods first and see if any blues are around," suggested Shandy. He jointed his slender Fiberglas rod and rummaged in his tackle box for a Sea Hawk—a red-and-yellow lure that looked like a small clothespin. There were two sharp treble hooks on it.

When they came out on the fantail with two folding chairs, Catfish slowed the *Albatross* so that the motor barely purred. The houseboat was moving at just the right speed for trolling. In a moment Catfish was looking over their shoulders.

"Who's steering the boat?" asked Jib, half alarmed.

"I hooked the wheel up to a rig I use as an automatic pilot," explained Catfish. "We got seventy-five miles to go before we reach Saint George Island. I'm letting the pilot do some of the work."

Catfish checked the prongs of their hooks to make sure they were good and sharp. "Can't say as it matters much to a blue," he said. "They feed fast and savage, but there's no sense of losing one. They always reminded me of those South American fish—piranhas. The ones that can strip the meat off a man or beast in minutes. Real mean little buggers."

He told them to troll about fifty feet of line and to keep jerking the lure. Shandy let the tip of his rod over the side and, with a flick of his wrist, shot the lure far astern. Jib did likewise from the other side of the cockpit.

The waves behind the *Albatross* kicked up a frothy white foam along their crests. They glittered aquamarine in the quick rays of reflected sun.

"Gulf's clear as an agate," murmured Catfish. "Jerk the tips of your rods so your lures get plenty of action."

The lures split the water five feet beneath the surface like frightened silver minnows darting through the boat's wake.

Suddenly Catfish let out a whoop. "There they are! A dozen of them, coming up fast. Work those rods, lads!"

Jib and Shandy felt strikes at almost the same time. The rods bent as if they had hooked bottom. The lines slashed through the water. Both boys pumped their reels, losing line when the fish plunged, gaining it when the blues darted for the surface.

"There he is!" shouted Shandy as a two-pound fish streaked through the froth with half a dozen others fighting to get the same lure it was already hooked to.

"Look at them after your lure! Reel in! Hurry before the school leaves!"

Jib's fish came aboard first, gleaming silvery blue as it flopped furiously on the deck. Jib put his foot on it to keep it from rolling up in the line.

"Watch those teeth," cautioned Catfish. "They're sharp as needles."

The three-pronged hooks were caught deep in the fish's jaws. Getting them out without getting either hooked or bitten was tricky.

"Yaow!" Jib yelped, dropping the fish and holding up his finger, where a drop of blood was quickly forming.

Catfish shook his head. "They're mean customers, all right."

Both fish were in and Shandy tossed out again, immediately hooking another. The blue raced off to the left of the *Albatross*. There was no letup on the run and the Fiberglas rod doubled up as the fish dove deep.

"Don't let him get under the boat!" Catfish warned.

But it was too late. The rod snapped straight and the line went slack.

"Cut on the bottom," said the captain. "You can't catch 'em all."

Jib was fighting in another fish, and as he lifted it dripping and thrashing over the side, the school suddenly peeled off and disappeared like flitting shadows.

In a frenzy of excitement, sea gulls screamed overhead. A school of baitfish panicked across the wake as they were intercepted by the blues. Hundreds of tiny fish leaped out of the water like drops of flashing silver, clinging in a brilliant cloud for an instant before dropping into the sea with a hiss like the sudden downpour of rain. Again and again it happened and the gulls dove screaming into the confusion, filling their beaks with the glittering fish while beneath the waters the savage blues carried on their fast, fierce onslaught.

"If the birds don't get 'em, the other fish do," remarked

Catfish as the violent waters finally calmed and left nothing more than a greasy slick. "It's the fight for survival."

The excitement of the moment passed and the school disappeared. The sea was quiet, the gulls flew off in the direction of the shore, and the boys trolled without getting any more strikes.

"That's the way they go," Catfish said. "One minute they're scrambling to get your bait and the next there isn't a fish within fifty miles of it."

"Why aren't they around all year?" Shandy asked, picking a clump of sea grapes off the tip of his rod.

"Bluefish are migrators. They travel a lot. You saw how fast they move. Well, they show up when the water temperature is right, usually in the spring and in the fall. Right now they're staying offshore because the surf is getting too warm for them. Remember how many we caught at the jetties last fall when it turned cold?"

The boys nodded. Shandy recalled that the jetties had been packed with fishermen catching blues out of the big waves as they crashed up the channel toward St. Andrews.

"It doesn't make any difference how cold it gets." Catfish ran his finger along the side of one of the bluefish. "When these varmints hit the white water, fishermen come out like coveys of quail, ready to do battle."

"How big do they get in Florida?" Jib asked.

"A two-pound fish is about average," replied Catfish. "They'll work the rollers in the surf if there isn't a lot of sand being kicked up. Sand in the water gets in their gills so they can't breathe. They'll usually stay away from a rough surf. Then if you want to catch them from shore you need a long, maybe ten-foot surf rod so you can reach over the breakers and drop your lure out where it's calm and the fish are feeding."

"If they travel a lot," said Shandy, "where do they go?"

"Some say they range around the Atlantic and the Indian oceans. In the fall the blues move south from somewhere up on the north Atlantic coast. They hit our eastern coast first. I suppose they follow the baitfish. By spring they've reached our Gulf coast and sometimes hang on in the bays and inlets for a spell. I have an idea—I don't know if there's any truth to it, but I figure some stay around the whole summer, out deep where the water is cool. Nobody knows for sure."

"Hey!" Jib pointed astern where his lure was trolling. Just under the surface a large black shape was following it. "It's a shark!" he yelled.

"Reel in fast," said Catfish. "That's no shark, that's a cobia. He'll tear your tackle to bits." The captain ducked into the cabin and came out with a large rod holding a reel as big as a can of beans. "This is more his size," he said. "Let's see if he'll take it."

Catfish loosened the big hook and pulled out three feet of wire leader. Then he opened the bait well the boys had been resting their feet on.

"He's still there," whispered Shandy, "and there's another behind him. They're following us."

Catfish fumbled in the bait well and brought out a silver mullet. He put the ten-inch fish on the hook.

Shandy noticed that in contrast to the colorless light-weight monofilament on his spinning reel, Catfish's line was heavy and light tan, the kind he knew most fishermen used in the surf because it didn't show up against the sand.

Satisfied that the hook was well concealed in the mullet, Catfish tossed it overboard and let the line play out.

"He's going away," Shandy said, disheartened as the dark fish dove out of sight.

"He just sees my bait," said Catfish. "Watch."

Under the control of the captain's thumb, the line moved gently off the big spool. Then suddenly it started disappearing at a faster rate. The boys leaned forward excitedly. The reel was whirring faster and faster.

"Got to let him get it all," explained Catfish. He waited a few seconds longer, then, with a quick movement of his thumb, flicked the reel's clutch lever. That threw it quickly into gear and locked the spool so that no more line would run free.

The nylon tautened. At the same instant Catfish reared back hard, making the thick rod bend in a slight arc. And suddenly everything happened at once.

Fifty feet behind the boat the water erupted. A fish almost four feet long shot straight up in the air, showering water. Catfish was almost jerked off his feet.

"He's hooked!" he said, and grunted as the big fish dropped back into the sea with a resounding smack that threw bucketfuls of water in all directions.

"One of you get forward and shut off the motor, quick!"

Shandy raced for the wheelhouse and cut the motor off.

The big fish angled away from the boat, taking line slowly from the braked reel as it went—fifty, seventy-five, a hundred feet, two hundred feet. Then far out, just under the sun-dappled surface, it turned and its black shape looked more than ever like a shark.

Beads of sweat stood out on Catfish's brow. "He'll go sixty pounds or better!"

The cobia stayed away from the drifting boat. Occasionally it seesawed the line back and forth as it ran first one way, then another. When this failed, it went deep with a tremendous rush and jerked like an angry bulldog.

Fifteen minutes later Catfish wound the reel and started gaining line. "He's tired," he said. "He can't last long."

Moments later the gaping mouth, flat head, and broad body of the fish appeared. As it broke the surface, it rolled on its side.

"Git the gaff," said Catfish.

Shandy brought the long hook out of the cabin.

Holding the thrashing rod in the crook of his right arm, Catfish reached down with the gaff in his left hand, sank the hook into the fish, and hoisted with all his might until the cobia flopped aboard.

"Whew." Catfish wiped his face. "I wouldn't want to do that again right away."

He squinted out behind the *Albatross*. "We'll see more of those fish," he promised, "a lot more." Then he turned to Shandy and Jib and said, "Outside of maybe tuna or chicken, I reckon there's no better eating than cobia. Leastways not in my book." He grinned. "Tonight we'll fix some golden-brown fish fingers. How's that sound?"

"Umm, boy!" they said. Without knowing it, they had worked up a whale of an appetite.

Pursuit

THE *Albatross* plowed on through the afternoon sea. The Gulf lost its bright colors and turned dark and choppy. Jib was at the helm, holding on course. Occasionally he stepped out on deck to wipe the sea spray off the windshield after it turned to white salt.

Catfish and Shandy worked in the stern, cleaning the fish for supper. As they opened up the stomach of the big cobia, Catfish pointed out what the fish had been feeding on.

"Those long things in his stomach are eels," he said.

"Some of them are alive!" exclaimed Shandy.

"If you look close," Catfish nodded, "you'll see that those wiggling things are baby eels. The cobia ate a mother eel and she gave birth to her young inside his stomach."

"Will they live?"

Catfish shook his head. "I'm afraid not." He scooped up the mass of young eels and threw them overboard. "In

44

the seas every creature has to look out for himself. Out of maybe millions of young borne by one mother fish, only a scant handful survive. They fight to get born and they fight to stay alive. That's the story of their lives."

"Gosh, I sure hope they make it," said Shandy, watching the baby eels swim away.

They skinned and cut the meat off the big fish in solid white slabs. Catfish wrapped each piece in foil and stored them in the icebox. Then they cleaned the bluefish and put them on ice beside the cobia.

Afterward Catfish unrolled the coastal geodetic chart for the northern Gulf and checked their position.

"When do you think we'll get to Saint George Island?" Shandy asked.

"Along about sundown. We lost some time fishing, but it won't make too much difference." He pointed to a line he had drawn on the chart. "Here's our course. We should see a flashing white light just south of Saint Vincent Island. That's where we pick up the West Pass channel between Cape Saint George and Saint Vincent."

Catfish said he was going to lie down and get some sleep. The boys were to keep the boat on its compass bearing until they sighted the light, then wake him up.

Shandy got his binoculars and went out on deck. All he could see of the shoreline on their left was a thin band of yellow, where the beach was, and a wider band of green above it that he guessed was pines and palm trees. He made his way forward to the wheelhouse and told Jib about the white light they were to watch for.

By late afternoon the sea was considerably rougher. The

boys took turns at the wheel. In a couple of hours they spotted the light. It was just a speck at first but it grew brighter as they got closer. Jib woke Catfish and he took over.

It was dark when they got to the light. Catfish switched on the *Albatross'* powerful spotlight. "Look sharp now for the red nun buoys that mark the channel," he said. "There's three miles of shoal water and breakers to starboard. We don't want to run aground."

They passed several of the channel markers and turned slightly to port. In the distance were two lights flashing green. Catfish lined them up so the *Albatross* would be well within the channel.

They were just offshore of St. Vincent Island when they went through the pass. Close to starboard was the growing black shape of St. George Island. They could hear the hissing sound of waves breaking on the beach.

"We're going to turn out of the channel here," said Catfish, slowly turning the boat's wheel. In the lee of the island the water was calm. The bow swung to starboard. "There should be a good spot just offshore where we can drop the anchor for the night."

Shandy and Jib went on deck to ready the anchor. In the spotlight they could see the shore drawing closer. Thick marshes stretched off to the right, a sandy beach went to the left.

Catfish slowed the motor, then slipped it into reverse to stop their forward motion.

"This looks all right," he yelled. "Drop the anchor."

Shandy and Jib shoved the iron flukes overboard. When they hit bottom the boys let the boat drift off a short distance so the anchor would lie flat, then snugged the hawser to a deck cleat. To keep the boat from swinging, Catfish tossed out a small anchor from the stern.

"That should do it," he said, straightening up and sucking in a deep breath of the fresh-smelling air.

Minutes later he dug out his cast-iron skillet and started to heat peanut oil for frying the fish. Shandy and Jib busied themselves peeling potatoes on the fantail. Catfish cut the cobia into finger-sized pieces, salted them well, and shook them up in a paper sack with corn meal. When the oil was hot the pieces were put in until the skillet was brimming with frying fish. Soon the crisp brown pieces were ladled out with the pancake flipper and allowed to drain on sheets of newspaper. Then came the potatoes, cut in slivers and french-fried. In no time a feast fit for a king was served up on a large platter. It was a regular mountain of golden-brown fish and sizzling hot potatoes. The crew dove in hungrily.

The boys ate until they couldn't eat any more. When they finished they pushed themselves away from the table, groaning with contentment. It was all they could do to gather up the dishes and wash them on the fantail. When that chore was over they sprawled out on deck and listened to the surf breaking on the beach somewhere in the distance. Catfish joined them and lit his pipe.

"How would you like to go after flounder tonight?" he asked.

They sat up. "Will the water be smooth enough?" asked Shandy.

"Close to the lee of Saint Vincent Island it should be. The tide's due to change around ten o'clock. We should go before then or the fish'll be moving out."

"Sounds like a great idea," Shandy said.

"Sure does," Jib agreed.

Catfish puffed on his pipe and sent a smoke ring curling off toward the dark outline that was shore. "It might be too bright," he said, glancing up at the half moon already lighting the water with a pale ivory glow. "Flounder can spot you in a second if it's not dark."

"We'd sure like to have a try at them anyway," Shandy said hopefully.

"All right." Catfish grunted and climbed to his feet. "I'll get the gig and rig up the light while you boys put in the skiff."

Shandy and Jib hurried forward and were unlashing the light boat when Shandy suddenly straightened up.

"Listen. What's that?"

"I don't—yeahhh, I hear it too." Jib glanced in the direction where Shandy was looking. Faintly at first, then stronger and louder the throbbing of powerful boat engines reached them.

Abruptly the pulsating sound stopped.

"That's funny," murmured Shandy.

"It was a boat or something, wasn't it?" asked Jib.

"I think so . . . but I don't see any running lights."

"Maybe we'd better tell Catfish."

"Wait a minute—there—there it is! See, just going across the path of moonlight!"

It was a big black cruiser and it was closer to them than they had thought. But there wasn't a light showing; the shape glided past and melted into the covering dim moonglow like a passing thunderhead. It happened so quietly, it was almost as if there had been nothing there in the first place.

A chill ran down Shandy's spine. In the splinters of moonlight reflecting against the cruiser's steep stern he thought he had glimpsed her name. He hoped with all his might he had read it wrong.

He grabbed Jib's shoulder. "Did you notice anything—anything maybe *familiar* about it?" he asked tensely.

Jib shook his head. "Uh-uh," he said. "But they were looking at us."

"What?"

"Sure, didn't you see those two flashes of light just back of the bridge? I think the moon shined off somebody's glasses—binoculars, maybe."

"Oh-oh. C'mon," said Shandy. "We gotta get Catfish fast."

The captain was on his hands and knees in one corner of the cabin, grunting and muttering as he struggled to slide a storage battery out from under one of the bunks.

"We just saw another boat," said Shandy urgently. "It was a black cruiser without any lights and the motors were shut off."

"And it just slipped by like that," added Jib breathlessly. "While somebody was watching us with binoculars."

Catfish got to his feet, frowning.

"I'm not positive," said Shandy quietly, "but I think I saw the name of it." He took a deep breath. "It was the *Raven,* from Panama City!"

Jib spun around to face his friend. "Hey, isn't that Mr. Scanlon's . . ." His voice trailed off when he realized that they both knew.

Without a word, Catfish put his flounder gig back up on the brackets again. "Maybe we'd better put off going after flounder," he said, "and get going after treasure. That boat out there is not on any fishing trip."

But when they came out on deck the captain realized it was too late to take the *Albatross* any farther that night. The moon was gone; the air was strangely still and heavy. Lightning streaked the sky to the west of them, and overhead the stars were being snuffed out like candles as a great black mantle of clouds crept in from the sea.

"I don't like the looks of it," murmured Catfish, sniffing the air. "I don't like the looks of it at all."

Storm Bound

In the night the *Albatross* rolled and pitched while rain fell in drops that sounded like golf balls on the roof of the cabin. The island protected them from the wind, but lightning flashed and thunder rolled until dawn. Then the storm let up and the rumbling moved off to the southwest.

"Just a passing squall," said Catfish when they got up. But the sun refused to come out and the sky remained a tent of dirty gray clouds.

"Lucky we got the Intercoastal Waterway to stay in," the captain commented after breakfast. "The Gulf'll be kicking up pretty bad for a spell. We'll put in at Carrabelle and gas up."

They hauled in the anchors and started the motor. The bay was shallow and choppy enough to hide the treacherous oyster bars that could rip open the bottom of a boat. But once the *Albatross* moved back into the deeper water of the channel between St. George Island and the mainland there was nothing to fear.

A few hours later they passed the tip of the island and crossed East Pass, then shortly afterward they were in the lee of Dog Island and moving into the channel that would take them upriver to Carrabelle.

When they pulled in to a small marina there were so many other boats that Catfish had a hard time finding a place to tie up. Most of the boats were small ones used by the oyster fishermen. Some were big white broad-beamed shrimpers with their brown nets hanging from the booms to dry. Others were charter cruisers, their long slender outriggers gently bobbing and nodding in unison as the *Albatross* slipped up beside the gas dock. Shandy and Jib quickly secured her with bow and aft hawsers to pier pilings.

"We won't be here long, but you boys can go ashore and stretch your legs a little if you like," said Catfish. "Just don't wander too far off."

Shandy and Jib promised they wouldn't. They climbed across to the pier and started along it to look at the other boats.

"Gee, my legs feel like rubber!" exclaimed Jib.

"Mine too. As if we were still on the boat." Neither of them could get over how solid the ground felt, how hard it was to take a step and not find the ground rising up to meet them like the deck of the houseboat.

They hadn't gone far when both of them suddenly stopped in their tracks. Tied up to the pier just ahead of them was a big black cruiser. In white letters across the stern were the words: RAVEN—PANAMA CITY.

The boys looked at each other. Then, without a word, they turned and raced back to the houseboat.

Catfish was on the stern, where a man was filling the fuel tanks with a long hose from the gas tank on the dock.

As they jumped aboard, Shandy motioned for Catfish to come up to the bow.

"What's wrong?" he asked.

"The *Raven's* here."

Catfish frowned. "You certain?"

"Positive," said Shandy. "She's tied up just a few boats ahead of us next to the pier."

"Did anybody see you?"

"I don't think so. We ran back fast as we could."

"What are we going to do now?" asked Jib.

Catfish stroked his beard thoughtfully. "We'll give 'em the slip if we can." He glanced back toward the stern. The man was pulling his hose back to the pump. "You boys go into the cabin. With all these boats around here I should be able to sneak us out of the marina without anybody being the wiser."

The boys did as he said, but it was a long time before they heaved a sigh of relief. And by then the *Albatross* not only had left the marina far behind, but was well on out the river channel.

They followed the channel for a mile until they came to a flashing red buoy in St. George Sound, then they angled to starboard and went to East Pass, skirting the western tip of Dog Island to pick up the string of channel markers that led them out into the Gulf.

The sea was still choppy from the squall the night before,

but overhead the sun was trying to bore through the overcast. The wind was with them out of the west and it was not long before they reached St. Marks, where they refueled again and started their long run toward what the charts showed as a flashing beacon off Waccasassa Bay, eighty-three miles south.

Late in the afternoon, Jib, who had climbed atop the cabin roof to keep Shandy's binoculars trained on the horizon to see if they were being followed, called down to Shandy.

"Look at those funny-colored clouds back of us. I've been watching them for the last few minutes and they're sure building up fast."

Shandy glanced up from some fishing tackle he was rigging. He was surprised to see the dirty yellowish clouds himself.

"They must be having a bad storm back the way we came," he said, shading his eyes to see better. "I'm glad we're not there now."

Just then Catfish stepped out of the wheelhouse. There was a worried expression on his face.

"The barometer's falling fast and the radio's so full of static I can't hear a thing," he said, making his way past Shandy to the stern.

He looked at the gathering storm clouds for a moment, then shook his head. "I hate to push the gal any harder, but we can't get caught in a gale out here either," he said.

"Maybe we could pull in to another marina until it goes by," Jib suggested as he climbed off the cabin roof.

Catfish swept his hand toward shore. "There isn't a

marina or a town along that coast for miles. And we can't chance going back to Saint Marks—not the way that storm's shaping up." The captain shrugged. "Looks like our best bet is to head for Dead Man's Cove and ride it out as Jib said. Question is, can we make it?" He squinted at the sky, then started for the wheelhouse to set the *Albatross* on its new course. Shandy followed him.

A few minutes later he came out with a rolled geodetic map under his arm. "C'mon in the cabin. I'll show you where we're going."

With the chart spread out on the table in front of them, he pointed out a small cove on the coast that looked a long way from everywhere, especially from where their plotted course showed them to be at that moment. There was nothing but tidewater swamps and mud flats along the shore.

"Gee, do you think we can make it to the cove?" asked Jib.

"Sure we can," said Shandy. "Everything's going to be all right."

But less than an hour later the clouds on the horizon were banked up low in the sky over the *Albatross*. They looked like smooth bunches of steel wool and the closer they got, the darker and quieter the Gulf became. Finally it turned a sickly purple color and the breeze died out completely. The water smoothed until it was slick as oil, so still it looked as if it were solid.

"Better snug down the skiff and get out the sea anchors," said Catfish.

The boys carried the gear out of the cabin and stacked

it on the forward deck where it would be handy. Then they went back to the wheelhouse.

"How far are we from—" Shandy started to ask when Catfish suddenly thumped the bulkhead with his fist to attract their attention.

"Yonder she comes!" he yelled.

The boys jumped out on deck. Off their starboard beam the wind cut a wide swath across the water. The surface came alive as if a giant school of minnows were being attacked from below.

When it hit them the houseboat heeled abruptly to port. The howl of the wind sounded like a freight train rounding a curve at top speed. A loud crash and clattering came from inside the cabin. The boys hurried back and threw open the cabin door. Dishes, pots, and pans rattled across the deck. Locker doors hung open. All the furniture had piled up on one side of the cabin and a sack of flour had tumbled off a shelf to explode in a great white cloud that was settling over everything.

They slammed the door and pulled their way along the railing to the wheelhouse. The wind tore at them fiercely.

Catfish was braced against the wheel trying to bring the bow of the *Albatross* into the gale. The boat wouldn't respond. She remained tilted heavily to port.

"Our blasted supplies have shifted," grunted the captain. "See if you can get out those storm anchors, Shandy. Jib, you push the cabin gear to starboard. Try to even the load. Can't get to the things below decks. That's where the trouble is."

Sheets of rain hammered the wheelhouse windows.

Shandy heaved open the door. Outside the sea had gone wild. Huge waves were piling up, their crests sliced off by the wind that drove them smashing into the starboard bulkheads.

"Be careful!" shouted Catfish, then there was nothing but the crash and hiss of the waves in Shandy's ears.

As he clung to the railing and fought his way forward to the deck winch, he glanced toward shore. He could hardly see it but it was there, closer than he thought—a dull strip of green barely visible above the jagged white teeth of surf.

His feet slipped on the deck, and twice he came close to losing his grip and being washed over with a big wave that flooded over the scuppers.

Once he got around the bulk of the winch, he took one look at the deck and his heart caught in his throat. The storm anchors and rope were gone—they had been washed overboard!

The only thing he could think of was the big boat anchor secured in the bow. Crouching, he started for it, keeping both hands on the railing while the water swirled around his knees.

Just as he reached the place where it was tied down ahead of the skiff, Shandy heard a sharp splintering crack behind him. He glanced back just in time to see the radio antenna collapse, the mast and wire disappear over the side.

He lunged for the anchor and clung to it, desperately tugging at the fastenings as wave after wave frothed over the deck. Finally he got it loose and shoved it to the bow. With a mighty effort he pushed it over. Not more than fifteen feet of rope went out before the iron flukes struck bottom.

Catfish stuck his head out of the wheelhouse and yelled over the shriek of the wind.

"Let out as much rope as you can! Tie it off at the bow ring!"

Shandy payed the thick rope out into the sea until the coil was gone. Then he moved back to where the anchor had been stowed and untied the bowline knot that held it to the deck T cleat. Bending the rope around the cleat to make sure he would have enough slack, he worked forward again with the loose end and quickly tied it in a bowline to the large iron ring at the bow. As soon as it was snug, he slipped the loop off the T cleat and the rope drew taut.

It swept out of the water, quivering under pressure. The bow slowly swung into the wind. Just as Jib yelled for Shandy to get back to the wheelhouse, a giant wave smashed into the *Albatross* head on. Shandy grabbed the railing. The houseboat's stubby bow rose halfway, then jerked abruptly as the mountain of water cascaded over. When Shandy opened his eyes and wiped the stinging salt water out of them, he stared in disbelief at the bow. The iron ring and the anchor rope were *gone!*

Shipwrecked

THERE WAS nothing on the deck but a small jagged hole in the planking to show where the ring had been. Shandy choked down his despair and fought his way back to the wheelhouse.

Catfish was struggling to keep the houseboat's bow pointed seaward. But it was hopeless. "What happened? Rope break?"

"It took the ring and everything!" gasped Shandy. "I lost it all."

"Wasn't your fault," said Catfish. "I should have known it was getting too old to take that kind of strain."

"What are we going to do now?" asked Shandy.

"I reckon just hold on as long as we can," said Catfish. "We're losing ground fast. Better get ready to abandon her."

"Abandon the *Albatross*?" the boy asked in surprise.

60

"We can't do anything against these waves," said Catfish. "She's shallow draft so we should get pretty close to shore before she runs aground. Trouble is, bottom runs out pretty far along this coast."

"But isn't there a thing we can do?"

"Just round up what things we can carry. Pack whatever food you can and don't forget to put on your life preservers. As soon as we hit bottom we'll get at the skiff and flip it over the side, then load things aboard off the stern."

Shandy didn't wait to ask any more questions. He hurried back to the cabin.

The bottom came up faster than they had expected. There was a loud crunching and then the *Albatross* ground to a halt. Sea water flooded over her decks; waves she had once been able to ride now swept over her bows and smashed mightily against the wheelhouse and cabin.

"Get the skiff before she goes adrift!" shouted Catfish as he splashed his way forward. The boys tugged themselves along the lee rail to join him.

They got the boat loose, but when they tried to turn it over a wave half filled it with water. It almost sank. They drew it back along the portside, where the cabin blocked the worst of the waves, and managed to empty it.

"There's a tarp under Shandy's bunk," Catfish told Jib. "Throw the blankets and clothes in it and fetch it."

Shandy held the skiff while the captain started after the motor and their maps.

"Don't forget the telescope," Shandy called after him. Catfish nodded.

When the food had been stored under the bow thwart and everything else they could carry was aboard, the three of them climbed in and the skiff nearly swamped. Jib and Shandy started bailing with their shoes while Catfish started the motor.

The first of the surf was not as bad as it looked. They rode the waves in for fifty yards before settling in the trough between two giant foam-flecked combers. When the one behind them curled over and crashed down, it washed over their stern. The motor sputtered and died as the skiff filled with water.

Fortunately they were within wading distance of the shore, so they climbed out and dragged the skiff toward a long mud flat not far off. All around them the surf was booming and hissing, and the undertow was sweeping the bottom so strongly they could feel it sucking out the sand from under their feet.

When they finally dragged the skiff up on the mud flat and bailed it out, they were so tired they sagged down in their tracks and stopped to catch their breath.

"Well," said Catfish, looking down the shore, "at least we're on solid ground, even if it is about the farthest from anywhere we could have landed."

"Where are we?" asked Shandy.

"Don't know exactly until I check the chart. But most of this coast is all the same—a mile maybe of tidewater swamp back of us. After that nothing but miles and miles of cypress swamps. I reckon the only thing we can do is leave the skiff and tote what we can to the timber. Maybe we can find dry enough ground to set up a camp."

"What about the *Albatross?*" asked Jib.

"The way she's wedged into the sand we don't have to worry about her going anyplace," said Catfish. "If the seas don't knock her apart maybe we can float her in for repairs when the storm lets up."

The three of them stared back gloomily at their stranded houseboat. Only the top of the wheelhouse and cabin showed over the raging surf. Shandy felt it was the last time he would ever see the *Albatross*.

"Let's check the beach," he said to Jib. "Maybe some of our things will wash in."

They got up and started along the shore. The mud flat was actually a long, slender bar. On one side the surf hammered without letup. But a few yards beyond the welt of mud was a sawgrass marsh with dark, quiet, brackish water. The tall grass seemed to go on forever.

They hadn't gone far when they suddenly discovered the mouth of a fair-sized creek. The bar was thicker at this place from silt that had washed out of the creek, but there was an opening wide enough for the skiff if they could drag it over the bar. They hurried back to tell Catfish what they had found.

He was elated. "If we can get the skiff through, it'll save us a heap of work," he said. "The tide's coming in faster than normal. It won't be long before this beach is awash. Let's give it a try."

They eased the boat back into the surf and dragged it up the flat to the mouth of the creek. There they seesawed it back and forth until it was over the bar and into the brackish water on the other side.

Catfish tried to start the motor, but it only sputtered. The boys picked up two pieces of driftwood that had floated into the marsh and used them to pole the skiff along the creek.

It was slow work, so each of them took turns pushing. In this way they inched along for almost a mile, following the creek as it snaked through the thickest kind of marsh. The wind whipped fiercely through the tall tough grass and occasionally rain fell in sudden heavy downpours. Overhead the sky had lost its yellowish tinge and now the thick layer of clouds looked like smoke. Once a whole flock of sea gulls flew overhead and circled, crying loudly as if they were lost. But they were only waiting for others that came soaring out of the west. Then they all swooped off as quickly as possible in the opposite direction from the storm.

Pretty soon the creek grew so narrow the boys could almost touch the green walls of grass on either side of them. Just as they reached the point where it was impossible to go any farther with the boat they saw timber: cypress, pine, and palmetto. Off to their left ran a great thicket of ti-ti, but they didn't intend to get into that. They could spend the whole night trying to hack a path into it and in the end it wouldn't take them anywhere.

They pulled the skiff up on firm ground and unloaded everything. Catfish pointed out a tall cypress tree and said that would be the best place to make camp until they got their bearings.

The first thing they did was cut a clearing with their

machetes, keeping a close watch for cottonmouth moccasins and coral snakes.

"The sooner we get everything dried out and under a shelter the better off we'll be. The two of you cut some saplings and palmetto fronds for a lean-to. I'll see what I can do about getting a fire going."

It didn't take the boys long to build the shelter, and by the time they finished Catfish had a fire blazing. As they crowded around it their wet clothes began to steam with the welcome warmth it offered.

"We ought to try and keep this fire going all night," said Catfish. "I'll let you boys scout around for more firewood while I dry out some of our other gear."

"Yes, sir," said Shandy.

The boys took their machetes with them and started off toward the dense jungle of moss-heavy cypresses and thick black vines that twisted and climbed through the trees like enormous black snakes. There was no sawgrass now, but on every little mound of earth waxy-leaved palmettos grew. They found that the spot they had picked for a campsite was an island of high ground with shallow branches of brownish water cutting around it like a moat, then reaching out into the swamp in a hundred different directions so that in some places there was dry land and in others the trees stood in the water. Thrusting up out of the ground and out of the muddy pools were cypress knees two and three feet high, the odd-shaped roots struggling upward in search of air. In the gloom of the swamp some of them looked like small huddled figures, while others resembled strange animals with humped backs, slender necks, and outstretched talons. There was nothing cheerful about the swamp.

Just as the boys sloshed across a particularly deep and foul-smelling gully of stagnant water, Jib asked, "Whatd'ya think our chances are of getting found, Shandy?"

Shandy didn't want to alarm his friend so he said, "We won't have to worry about it. As soon as we want, we'll fix up the *Albatross* and everything'll be just as good as before."

"But what if the houseboat breaks up?"

"It won't," Shandy said with determination. "Not the old *Albatross*. Besides, aren't we always looking for some excuse to go camping, Jib? Gosh, we always talked about wanting to be shipwrecked on some desert island like Robinson Crusoe . . . and now here we are!"

"That sure doesn't make me want to be here as long as Robinson Crusoe," said Jib with certainty.

The boys searched until they found an old cypress that had toppled onto a dry hump of ground. They broke off dry branches from the underside of the tree until they had as much as they could carry, then they found their way back to camp.

Catfish had hung the blankets and spare clothes on green bamboo poles he had cut from a swale near the ti-ti, and these items were steaming beside the fire as they approached.

"Thought I'd get this stuff dried out while the rain's stopped," he said. "Did you see anything interesting back there?"

"Nothing but trees and swamp," said Shandy. "It looks as if nobody has been around here for a hundred years."

"Probably nobody has," said Catfish, feeling the blankets to see how they were coming. "And I don't reckon there's anybody around for a hundred mile either."

"Oh, gosh," Jib moaned.

"Don't worry now. The sea'll be kicking up its heels for a couple days but then it'll calm down and we can get out to the *Albatross* and see what damage has been done. By the way, anybody feel like eating?" he asked.

Jib brightened instantly. "I could eat a horse!" he exclaimed.

"I guessed maybe you could," said Catfish good-naturedly. "Let's see what we can find." He got up and went to the lean-to.

In two minutes he was back and he was not smiling.

"Did anybody think to bring water?"

"*Water?*"

The word stunned them into remembering that they had forgotten the most important thing of all. Every drop of fresh water they had was abroad the *Albatross*.

"And that's not all," added Catfish. "It looks as if our supper is going to be just beans and sardines."

"But what about the spaghetti, sugar, bread?" asked Jib.

"The waterproof bag held all right," said Catfish. "But something else didn't. Smells like vinegar to me."

Jib swallowed hard two or three times. Having to go without water was one thing, but having all that good food ruined by vinegar made him bite his lip to keep back the tears.

"Now, now," soothed Catfish. "It's not as bad as all that. There's plenty of canned things—even if most of the labels did get soaked off. And, shoot, as far as the water goes we can start by staking out a tarp in the clearing and catching some rain water."

Jib blinked his eyes rapidly. "Sure, that'd probably work, wouldn't it?" He grinned. "I forgot all about those canned things."

The boys took the dry blankets and clothes off the bamboo poles and used their machetes to cut the sticks into three-foot lengths for staking the tarpaulin in an opening beyond the trees. Meanwhile Catfish opened three cans of beans and sardines and set them beside the fire to heat.

When the food was sizzling in its containers and the aroma almost more than they could bear, they nudged the cans out of the coals to cool and fell to with a vengeance. The meager supper only whetted their appetites for more.

Finally Catfish smacked his lips and allowed that it didn't seem right for them to starve themselves in view of all they had gone through. So in short order he dug out three cans of Vienna sausages and a big can of turnip greens and they feasted all over again.

After supper they built up the fire and lay back on their blankets in complete comfort. As it grew dark the wind gradually slackened and they became aware of the sounds of the swamp. At first the peeper frogs opened up with a shrill chorus, then the crickets joined in. Once the chirping and the peeping were in full swing, leopard frogs near the creek added their scratchy-throated voices. And from a long way off, coming in gradually like bass drums bringing up the end of a parade, the bullfrogs started booming their deep hollow notes that beat time for all the rest. With the lulling sounds of the swamp and the comforting warmth of the fire, it wasn't long before the tired castaways were fast asleep.

Castaways

THE NEXT MORNING Shandy awoke to the sound of thousands of birds chirping and calling as they greeted the morning and rustled in the trees of the swamp. He rolled over and sat up. A thin wisp of smoke curled up from the gray ashes of the fire. Overhead the sky was lead-colored with no sign of a sun. He thought he could hear the steady pounding of surf in the distance but he wasn't sure. It hadn't rained during the night and the tarpaulin was as dry as it had been when they staked it out. He licked his lips and wished he had a drink of water.

Across the fire from him Jib stirred, then suddenly jerked upright and stared about.

"Gosh, for a minute I though I was having a nightmare." He rubbed his neck and made a face. "Boy, this ground is awful hard."

70

Catfish woke up yawning and looked about at the gray strangeness of the swamp.

"Can't see that there's been any change in the weather," he said.

"I'm thirsty," said Jib.

"Reckon we all are," said Catfish. He climbed to his feet and stretched. "The first thing we're gonna do is get us some drinking water."

"How are we going to do that?" asked Shandy. "Jib and I didn't see anything that looked like a spring when we went after firewood yesterday. And the creek has salt water mixed in it."

"Don't worry. As long as we got machetes we always got good clear drinking water in a swamp—not much, mind you, but enough to take the edge off our thirst until we find something better."

"Well, I'm sure for it then," said Shandy. He didn't want to mention breakfast but the thought of food had already put a hollow ache in his stomach. He knew that what little they had salvaged wasn't enough to last long, so he tried to put the thought of eating out of his mind.

"First off," said Catfish, "you and Jib collect the cans we opened last night and wash them out at the creek. You can forget those that had sardines in 'em—there's nothing that can kill that smell. Just get the others."

The boys picked up the cans and went down to the creek while Catfish made the camp more "shipshape," as he called it. The blankets were folded and stacked well back inside the lean-to. The fire was replenished with dry sticks and fanned until it blazed brightly once again, adding at least a small touch of cheer to their dismal day.

When the boys came back from the creek with the washed cans Catfish said, "All right, now let's see if we can find us some drinking water."

Getting a good bearing on their campsite by lining it up with a tall lightning-scarred cypress in one direction and a peculiarly twisted water oak in the other, he led the way into the swamp in the direction the boys had taken when they went after firewood.

Ten minutes later they stopped in a cluster of tall trees and stunted palmetto undergrowth.

"This looks like as good a place as any," said Catfish.

The boys looked around them for a spring. The ground was carpeted with soggy dead leaves. Here and there cypress knees thrust their heads up into the dim light filtering through the thick foliage far above them. Long, twisted black vines draped and looped their way to the ground from branches high overhead.

"But—there isn't anything to drink here," said Jib.

"I wouldn't bet on that if I were you," said Catfish, grinning broadly. He reached up and grasped a shaggy vine as thick as his arm and hauled it down to the ground. Holding it there with his foot, he then reached up, swung the machete twice, and hacked a neat two-inch wedge out of the tough, fibrous wood at the height of his chest.

"Now set the cans on the ground near my foot," he instructed.

As soon as they did, Catfish bent down, swung the

machete again, and severed the vine at an angle near his foot. Grabbing the freshly cut end, he quickly held it over a can. A steady stream of clear water trickled out.

"Gee whiz, would you look at that!" said Jib.

"Have all of the vines got water in them like that?" asked Shandy.

Catfish nodded. "The thickest ones have the most. The sweetest water you ever set your lips to."

"Gosh, we'll never have to go thirsty!" said Jib excitedly. "There's vines all over the swamp."

"Right," said Catfish. "But they're slow putting out water. You fellas drink that and I'll cut vines for the other cans, then we'll see if we can find some swamp cabbage."

"One thing still puzzles me," said Shandy. "Why did you cut the notch in the vine?"

"That's to let air in so the water'll come out faster."

"Why sure," said Shandy. "I should have thought of that."

Twenty minutes later they had sampled the water from several vines until everyone's thirst was satisfied. Then they were ready to search for something to eat.

"This time we're going to have to do a little more work," said Catfish as he led them back to the edge of the tidewater swamp where the timber left off and the marsh began.

They followed him in single file, keeping to the highest ground wherever possible and skirting the fingers of brackish water that branched out from the creek and flooded the unbroken prairie of coarse shoulder-high sawgrass. Along the fringe of this marsh the ground was spongy underfoot.

Without the protective shade of the trees the growth was lush and thick. Catfish hacked a trail for them through the larger palmetto scrub and the giant elephant-ear plants with their broad three-foot-long leaves, advancing cautiously each step of the way. All of them knew this was cotton-mouth-snake and alligator country. It was no place to be in a hurry.

In a few minutes Catfish found what he was looking for —a young palm that wasn't much taller than he was. With several sweeps of his machete he lopped off a number of the long sharp-tipped fronds so that they could get closer to the tree without getting scratched.

"I've never eaten a swamp cabbage," said Jib. "Or seen one either," he added.

"Well, take a good look at it then," said Catfish, pointing at the six-inch-thick trunk of the palm tree.

"Huh?" Jib stared. "You mean it grows in trees?"

"This kind does," said Catfish. "That's why they call this particular kind of tree a cabbage palm. It's really the bud of the tree and it's inside the trunk up there near the top. Now I'll show you how to get it."

With several healthy swipes of the machete he cut off the palm's upper fronds. Then he hacked through the fibrous trunk about three feet down from the top.

This piece he laid on the ground and began splitting it lengthwise, cutting toward the center a little at a time and peeling the tough outer layers from the stalk one by one. Each layer was more tender than the one before it.

"What we're after is the choice meat right in the center," Catfish explained. "That's the heart of the palm."

"Gee, it comes apart just like big stalks of celery," said Jib.

"They're a lot alike," said the captain, taking out his jackknife. "Now that the toughest part is off, you start taking it easy 'cause you're getting close to the part you want to eat." He slit several more layers away from the stalk and finally held up what was left. It was as big around as his arm.

"There's your swamp cabbage," he said. "You can cook it or eat it raw." He sliced off a couple of pieces for the boys.

Jib took a bite and chewed it thoughtfully. "Gosh, it tastes a lot like . . . well, kinda like cabbage and celery both at the same time."

The captain chuckled. "They tell me that in some of those fancy expensive restaurants in south Florida people pay a pretty penny for it. They call it 'heart of palm salad.' " He squinted along the marsh. "There's enough cabbage palms around here to last us a year."

"A year!" Jib exploded.

"Just a figure of speaking," Catfish hastily assured him. "Shucks, I aim for us to be long gone from here before we get our fill of swamp cabbage."

"Is this our breakfast?" asked Jib, looking expectantly at the stalk Catfish was wrapping up again in one of the fibrous outer layers he had peeled off.

"Part of it," the captain said. "The rest I reckon we got to look for on the coast. There's a cast net stowed in the skiff. What say we pole back to the Gulf and try to find some mullet? Nothin' in the world can beat fresh-roasted mullet and swamp cabbage, you know."

"That's a good idea," said Shandy. "Maybe we can find out how bad off the *Albatross* is."

"Right. But don't get your hopes up too high," said Catfish. "I got a sneakin' suspicion we're not going to like what we'll see."

The captain was right.

When they reached the mouth of the creek and beached the skiff on a sand bar, the *Albatross* was a discouraging sight.

The pounding waves had pushed her closer to shore but she was tilted at a dangerous slant, with half her deck underwater. Catfish said that was probably caused from her hull digging into the bottom along the port side and the waves washing mud and sand up under her starboard side. The sea was still so rough it was difficult to tell whether or not the engine compartment was completely flooded, but at that distance it looked as if there was little hope. The captain took off his cap and shook his head gloomily.

"Maybe the hull will be all right," he said in an effort to reassure the others. "She's good sturdy timber." But he was worried about the surf. He could see it was still breaking over the high side of the boat. He knew that if it didn't cut down soon it wouldn't be long before the cabin and the wheelhouse would be torn loose.

"Shouldn't we get some kind of signal fire going on the shore to attract attention?" asked Shandy.

"Sure," said Jib eagerly. "Maybe back in the woods there's a fire tower somewhere and they'd come to our rescue."

Catfish shook his head. "Afraid I'll have to say no on both counts, boys. In the first place, Jib, there aren't any towers or they'd be marked on the chart. And in the second place, Shandy, our signal fire might attract the kind of varmints we don't want, if you get my meanin'."

"I guess you're right," admitted Shandy. "If Mr. Scanlon's after the scope, we sure don't want to make it easy for the *Raven* to find us."

"Well, gee whiz," said Jib, "then who *is* gonna rescue us?"

"There's a fair chance that some of the Air Force patrol planes'll be flying along the coast. Maybe even looking for boats in trouble like ours. There's a big base at Tampa, you know."

Shandy shaded his eyes and looked at the *Albatross*. "Is there any way we could fix the radio?"

"Afraid not. We lost the whole aerial. Besides," said the captain, "it's just a receiver, not a transmitter. Even if we could get her to working, about the most we'd pick up would be the weather reports and maybe some shrimpers working out of Saint Marks."

"Do you suppose we could get out to her in the skiff yet?"

"Not with that surf. We'd swamp before we got four boat lengths from the beach. Long as it doesn't get any rougher, I figure the *Albatross*'ll hold her own. The worst that could happen would be that she broke up."

"Gee—then there wouldn't be anything for anybody to find," said Jib.

"I don't think it'll come to that," said Catfish, glancing down the coast. "For now, let's get that cast net and see if the storm washed any mullet over the bar into the marsh."

They hauled the large rolled net out of the locker in the bow of the skiff, and as they walked along the welt of sand piled higher by the storm, Catfish untangled the meshes from the heavy lead weights and untwisted it.

They had not walked far when they came to a broad opening in the sawgrass that made a natural pocket for the still water it sheltered. Unlike the creek, which was stained deep brown from dead vegetation, this water had been washed by the sea and was much clearer.

Catfish kicked off his sneakers and rolled his pants up to his knees. Then he placed the center of the net in his teeth so that the weights hung down and he could use both hands to fold it in layers on his left arm. When he was all set he took one edge in his right hand and, holding the net in front of him, waded into the opening.

The water was only a couple of feet deep and he slowly moved forward, turning his head from side to side and scanning the smooth surface in front of him.

"Do you see any mullet?" yelled Jib as the captain neared the sawgrass on the opposite side.

Catfish didn't answer, but they saw that he was intently watching something between himself and the sawgrass. He shuffled forward a few feet, then abruptly twisted and swung the net up and forward, spreading it at the same instant he let go with his teeth.

It swirled through the air fully open and struck the water with a flat hissing sound, the weights dragging the edges quickly to the bottom.

He splashed to it, grabbed the center again, and drew it toward him. The net closed as it came out of water. The boys saw several long silver fish entangled in the meshes. Looking pleased over the result of his cast, Catfish waded back to the bar to remove his catch.

"That must take awfully strong teeth," said Jib.

"Reckon it does," agreed Catfish, handing him an edge of the net so he could feel the weight of the barrel leads strung closely around the bottom. "There's enough weight to pull out every tooth in your head if you forget to let go."

The captain left his catch on the bar and straightened out his net again. Then he waded back into the marsh flat and made two more casts that provided them with enough fish to last the rest of the day.

The boys strung the mullet on a long tough blade of sawgrass and hung them over the side of the skiff. Then they poled back up the creek to eat breakfast at camp.

It was shortly after they had eaten that Catfish brought up the idea of a guard detail.

"What do we have to guard against?" asked Jib.

"Against getting rescued," said Catfish. "We're a good stretch away from the houseboat. If somebody came to investigate her we wouldn't know about it back here in the timber. We've got to set up a watching post down there on the beach."

"Now that the storm's over, couldn't we move the camp to the sand bar?" asked Shandy.

Catfish rubbed the stubble of his beard thoughtfully. "The waves aren't washing across it any more, but the tide was out this morning. With it in, there wouldn't be enough room for us and our gear too. And not for a lean-to either."

Shandy snapped his fingers. "Wait a minute, I got an idea! You said we couldn't use a signal fire because it might attract the *Raven*, right?"

"Right," agreed the captain.

"Okay, so we don't use any fire on the bar at night and we don't use any fire by day—unless we *know* we're not attracting the *Raven*."

Catfish scratched his head. "Better say that again, lad. I think I lost you."

"Yeah," put in Jib, "how're you gonna know who sees your fire, tell us that."

"Easy," said Shandy. "We've got binoculars, haven't we?"

"Sa-a-a-y, that might work after all," said Catfish. "You mean we light the signal fires only if we see a plane, or a boat that isn't the *Raven*?"

"Sure. Mr. Scanlon's boat is a black cruiser; we'd know it a mile away, wouldn't we? And with the glasses we could be double sure. With one of us taking turns on the beach from daylight to dark, we'd know right away if anybody else came along."

"Hey, yeah," said Jib. "Maybe we could even fix up the motor and use it on the boat for changing guards."

"And to carry wood down for the fire—three fires, that's always a distress sign."

Catfish slapped his knee. "By golly, what are we waitin' for!"

Throughout the afternoon the boys trudged back and forth between the timber and the boat, loading the skiff high with dry wood for the fire, then green wood to make lots of smoke. In the meantime Catfish dismantled what he could of the outboard motor and carefully wiped off each piece before putting it back together again. Finally he looked up and said:

"I'll take the first load down tonight and get it all ready for morning."

"Maybe one of us better go along to help," said Shandy.

"Nope. I get the first watch. I can sleep in the skiff on the bar and be up before dawn. Then I'll come back to camp around eight o'clock, we'll have breakfast, then you fellas can go down. How's that sound?"

The boys agreed that it was a good arrangement.

So that evening, after eating the last of the mullet, Shandy gave the captain his binoculars and the boys watched him pole the skiff into the darkness of the creek.

"See you in the morning," he called. Then the outboard coughed and sputtered several times, but finally it caught and came to life with a roar that echoed through the swamp.

The boys let out a happy yell and stayed on the bank listening until the sound of the motor slowly faded away in the distance. Then they went back to the big cypress and built up the fire until it was crackling cheerfully and casting a warm, cozy light around their comfortable camsite.

"Y'know," said Jib as he sprawled on his blanket and stared into the glowing embers, "being out here and all . . . it's not really so bad after all, is it, Shandy?"

From the other side of the fire Shandy said drowsily, "I wouldn't give anything to be anyplace in the whole wide world but right here." And he meant it.

Never Trust
a Whooping
Crane

THE BIRDS in the trees were squawling in fine voice when Shandy woke up and saw something that made him think he was still dreaming. Catfish was squatting beside the fire, roasting a big bird.

"Where'd you get that!" he blurted out.

"Shhhh," the captain glanced quickly at Jib's round form rolled up in his blanket and snoring soundly. "I caught him in the marsh this morning," he whispered. "He had a broken wing. He's a sea gull."

"A sea gull!"

Catfish winced and jerked a warning finger to his lips. "Not so loud, boy."

Shandy dropped his voice. "What's the matter?"

"Well, Jib here might not be too fond of sea gull. Reckon we could pass it off as a duck?"

"He might know the difference— it's kinda big."

"Ummm, you're right." Catfish furrowed his brow while he slowly turned the bird on its spit. In a moment his eyes narrowed. "Maybe we could call it a rare kind of duck, one that's bigger than usual."

"Do you know any rare-duck names?"

"Not offhand." Catfish thought awhile. "How about cock-ah-vin-de-boozy?"

"Wow, that's a beaut!" said Shandy in admiration. "What is it?"

"It's French for a kind of bird, I think. I read it on a menu in New Orleans. Got a nice ring to it, hasn't it?" The captain held his nose and said it again. "That's the way it's really supposed to sound."

"Well, I guess if Jib's never had it before it won't make any difference."

Catfish pricked the bird with the point of his knife to see if it was done. "Breakfast is ready," he announced.

"Wake up, Jib! Look what we got," called Shandy, mustering what enthusiasm he could.

A corner of the blanket quivered and dropped. One of Jib's eyes peered out, blinking owlishly at what Catfish was holding proudly in front of him.

Then the boy shot out of his blanket, fully awake. "Golly gee, where'd you get the turkey?"

"It's not a turkey, it's a duck, kinda like." Then the captain hastened to tell them how he saw the bird flopping through the sawgrass, chased it in the skiff, and finally caught it.

Jib leaned down and whiffed the aroma from their breakfast. "Mmmm," he murmured, twitching the end of his nose. "What kinda duck is he?"

Shandy glanced quickly at the captain.

"He's a cock-ah-vin-de-boozy," said Catfish without blinking an eye.

"Oh." And that was all Jib said. He took a final sniff, then Catfish carved the bird and passed out steaming portions of the dark meat to each of them.

Jib put his teeth to a drumstick and went through it as if it were an ear of corn. The rest of his share disappeared equally fast. When he fiinshed he smacked his lips and looked up.

"Boy," he said, "if I didn't know better I'd say that tasted just like the goose we always have at Grandpa Duke's every Christmas. You don't reckon geese and these boozy birds are kin to each other, do you?"

"I wouldn't be surprised," said Catfish in all seriousness. "Leastways they might be kissin' cousins somewhere down the line."

Shandy didn't say anything but he reckoned he wouldn't be much for one of Grandpa Duke's geese if they were. The sea gull tasted mighty fishy to him.

"Now that everybody's got a full stomach," said Catfish, "I've got another surprise for you. The surf's down and now the outboard's workin' we can take a run out and see about the *Albatross*."

"That's great!" Both boys jumped to their feet, ready to go.

"Not so fast," said Catfish. "We're gonna be hot and

thirsty getting there, so we'll need to take plenty of water with us."

"We'll have to go back farther in the woods than we went yesterday," Jib said. "We used up all the water from the vines there."

"There'll be plenty more," Catfish assured him. "That's one of the reasons I want to get out to the *Albatross*. Those five-gallon jerry cans of drinking water we stowed under the deck should still be all right. But to be on the safe side we hadn't better count on that."

They gathered their empty cans and the machetes and started into the timber. Catfish was right, they didn't have to go far beyond the place they had collected water the day before to find more vines. They filled all their cans, then experimented with one of the plastic food bags to see if it was strong enough to hold water. Shandy was just about to shinny up a tree and pull down a particularly large vine when he suddenly heard Jib gasp.

"Hey!" he exclaimed. "There's somebody standing over there!"

"What!"

"Look there. See? He just came out of that bunch of ti-ti."

Catfish and Shandy looked where he was pointing. Sure enough, it was a man. He had his back to them and it looked as if he was waving a handkerchief over his head.

They let out a yell, then started running toward the man as fast as their legs would carry them. He was some distance off and on the far side of a big brackish tidal slough, but none of them stopped to go around for fear of losing him.

They splashed straight through, going almost up to their waists, but jumping like kangaroos every chance they got in case of snakes or, worse, alligators. Catfish fell down twice but bounced right back up again, with mud oozing down his face and water squirting out of his sleeves.

When they dashed up the opposite bank they saw the stranger grab for a long red-and-white-striped pole and half turn, as if undecided whether to run or stand his ground.

"Wait!" yelled Shandy, waving.

When they skidded to a halt in front of him, the man's eyes were as big as apricots.

"Well I'll be—!" he sputtered. "What in tarnation y'all doin' way out here?"

Wheezing, Catfish quickly explained what had happened to them and how they had been living off the swamp ever since the storm. While Catfish talked, the man wiped his perspiring face with his handkerchief, and through thick gold-rimmed glasses that magnified his eyes he stared at them, shaking his head in disbelief. Shandy noticed that he looked almost as ragged as they were. He wore high-top boots laced up only halfway, and rolled-up baggy pants with the knee out of one of the legs. His khaki shirt had only two buttons left; safety pins pinned it together where they were missing.

"We thought we were miles from people," said Catfish, finally catching his breath. "How come you're out in this wilderness?"

The man peered over the frames of his thick glasses at them. Then he grinned. In a low voice, as if he were letting them in on a very important secret, he said, "I don't reckon you would know about us. We're a special survey party for the U. S. Gov'ment."

"There's more than you?"

"Ahah—whole crew's comin' back up the line." The stranger jerked his thumb over his shoulder, and for the first time they noticed a wide jagged tunnel that funneled back through the ti-ti behind him. It was cut through brush so thick and tall that the branches made solid walls that curved up and almost came back together overhead.

"Did you cut that all by yourself?" said Shandy.

"Yep." The stranger tapped the handle of the machete dangling at his belt. Shandy stared down the long trough, and at the far end he could see another man beating at the air with a handkerchief.

The stranger stuck out his hand. "Name's Plumbad," he said. "Levert A. Plumbad." Catfish introduced the boys and himself and they shook hands.

"Yessiree," said Mr. Plumbad, puffing out his safety pins a little. "Me an' my men are surveyin' what I reckon will be the longest, the most important, and the most secret topo line in the entire history of the United States Gov'ment Engineer Corps. Neighbor, it will run from north Georgia to here and from here all the way down the coast of Florida and back up the other side, where it gets tied in with another line run some years ago."

"What in the world does the government want with anything that long?" asked Catfish.

Mr. Plumbad chuckled and looked over his glasses at Catfish. "Wish I could tell you, neighbor, but you know how these gov'ment things are. Ain't allowed to tell even the men in my crew, it's that secret."

The more Jib tried to follow the conversation, the more confused he was. Finally he spoke up and asked Mr. Plumbad what a topo line was.

The surveyor said "Ahah" again and said he reckoned he could tell that much. He took a deep breath. "It's for mapping out things, sonny. It's so the Engineers can tell where to go for building—ah, whatever it is they want to build. Now us, we come out here and put down stakes in the ground, see, with tacks in the top of them, and then mark down in a book exactly where we put them. Maybe fifty or a hundred years from now somebody gets around to wantin' a road or somethin' built out here, well all they got to do is look up in the book to see where our stakes got drove and then they come hunt them up again, d'ya follow me?"

"I guess so," said Jib slowly. "But how come those stakes aren't turned to dust by then?"

"Smart boy," said Mr. Plumbad. "Most of them are," he went on. "But them that ain't they can start off from and figure where the rest were with a survey instrument which is really nothing but a compass. You see, even if the stake's gone the important thing is the tack. I reckon I've spent thirty year lookin' up tacks that was lost. Some worn away thin as a thistle, too, but I found 'em. Yessiree, when the gov'ment sends Levert A. Plumbad out to find a tack, he comes back with a tack."

"And then they can build the road or whatever, is that it?" asked Catfish.

"Shucks no, neighbor. That's what they supposed to do," said Mr. Plumbad. "But most the time those old lines are way off or somebody wants somethin' changed and we end up surveyin' 'em all over again."

At that moment another man came out of the tunnel, carrying a cloth sack over one shoulder and an ax over the other. He was dressed like Mr. Plumbad but he was taller and skinnier. In fact, Shandy thought he had never seen such a skinny man in his life.

"This here's my stake setter, Angus Hatfield," said Mr. Plumbad. "Angus, say howdy to Mr. Jackson and the boys."

"Howdy," said Angus.

"Ahah. He don't talk much," said Mr. Plumbad, chuckling. "Been on this job too long, I reckon. Ain't used to bein' around people."

"How long have you fellas been out here?" asked Catfish.

Mr. Plumbad lifted his cap and scratched his forehead with his little finger. "Le'see, now," he frowned. "We started this line 'bout a year ago come July. Been in these parts now maybe three, four months. Reckon they done forgot about us in Mobile, Hatfield?"

"Reckon," said Hatfield.

"Mobile, Alabama?"

"Yep. That's where our gov'ment headquarters is—or was, if they ain't moved it in the last year." Mr. Plumbad cocked his head and looked off at nothing in particular.

Behind him two other men stalked out of the thicket. One was short with milk-bottle shoulders. He was carrying what looked to Shandy like a short brass telescope fastened to three long legs. He was having trouble keeping all of the legs off the ground at the same time. The other man was almost twice the first one's size and he carried another one of those candy-cane-striped poles with him.

When they appeared, Mr. Plumbad seemed to come back from wherever he'd been and said the fella with the telescope was his instrument man, Bill Zeffer, and the other one was Yank, his rear rod man.

The newcomers nodded when they were introduced, then they moved off to one side and started removing ticks from their clothing.

The boys could tell that they expected Mr. Plumbad to do their talking for them. And he did. He whispered to Catfish that Bill Zeffer was the only instrument man in the world who could sight a string in straw grass three-quarter mile away, but he was so farsighted that if you were to stand his instrument side by side with Skinny Hatfield you would have to show him which was which. Then he slapped his leg and said "Ahah, ahah" a couple of times and jerked his thumb at the big one he called Yank.

"He's from Mitchigan. A Northner. Don't pay him no mind when he opens his mouth," Mr. Plumbad warned. "He don't talk like folks yet." And the surveyor gave Catfish and the boys a good-friend look over the top of his glasses.

"Say, why don't y'all come down to our camp?" said Catfish. "We're just across the slough a piece and maybe you fellas can help us figure a way out of here."

"Be our pleasure," smiled Mr. Plumbad. Turning to his crew he said, "How far back is Lucas and Scuffmore?"

"About two mile, reckon," spoke up the instrument man.

"You've got more men with you?"

"Just two more," said Mr. Plumbad. "They're measuring the line with a chain. They almost caught up to us last week but they missed a turn and went a mile off course. Like as not to found them if we hadn't sent someone back to see where they was."

"Where do you put up for the night, anyway?"

"Oh, we keep bringing up the truck and camp out wherever we are, towns being so far off and all. The driver just stump-hops along till he finds us."

"Through *this* timber?"

"Yep. He comes right down the line. Never was much of a truck nohow."

On the way back to camp everyone skirted the slough, and when they reached the other side they collected their water supply, then headed for the big cypress.

Just as they approached the marsh, Mr. Plumbad whirled and cocked his head. "Hush!" he cried. "Hear that?"

"Hear what?" asked the instrument man.

"Hatfield?"

"Nope."

Mr. Plumbad didn't bother to ask the Yank, but he answered without being asked.

"Sounded like a blue heron," he said.

Right away Shandy knew the man had said the wrong thing. Mr. Plumbad's face got as red as Georgia clay, and the look he gave the Yank would have shriveled a prune.

"That's a whoopin' crane!" sputtered Mr. Plumbad. "The rarest bird in the whole world!"

"Gosh," murmured Jib, awed.

"Yessiree," said Mr. Plumbad. He put his hand to his mouth and went "WhhhooOOP! WhhhooOOP!" Then aside to the boys he said that that was their mating call. "Only fifty-two of them birds knowed to exist—all took care of by your United States Gov'ment," he said, stretching his safety pins again. "Yonder is the fifty-third bird. WhhhooOOP! WhhhooOOP!"

The sawgrass rustled and up flew a large blue heron.

"Gosh," said Jib again. But then he didn't know the difference.

When they reached camp, Catfish started getting out some of their canned food for lunch. Mr. Plumbad's face was still just a shade lighter than a ripe tomato but he managed to tell Catfish to save what they had, there were plenty of supplies in their truck and he reckoned that if Yank was smart enough to fetch them without getting lost. then they were welcome to share what they had.

As soon as the man left, Mr. Plumbad sagged into a heap under the cypress tree. "If ever—ever again I have my druthers," he swore, "I'd druther never meet up with another *Yankee*!"

And everyone could see that he meant it.

To Salvage
the
Albatross

It was an hour or so later when a horn honked back in the timber. Hatfield nudged the instrument man, Bill Zeffer, and the two of them went off in the direction of the honking.

"As long as there's an emergency," said Mr. Plumbad, "I don't reckon the gov'ment will mind us not working for a while to see if we can help you boys out."

Catfish said that was mighty kind of them but he didn't know what could be done, unless there was a chance of saving the *Albatross.*

"You never can tell," said Mr. Plumbad. "This crew of mine ain't much for words, but when it comes to getting something done, they don't waste no time about it."

In a few minutes the men came back, carrying a big wooden box between them. Yank brought up the rear with a water keg on his shoulder. Everyone gathered around for dinner.

The box was packed with canned food, onions, cheese, and loaves of bread. Each man took three cans of sardines, two of Vienna sausages, an onion, a slab of cheese, and a loaf of bread. Shandy thought they were making sandwiches for everyone, but they weren't. They were only making their own.

"Don't be bashful," said Mr. Plumbad. "Grab yourself some things and make some sandwiches."

"Where did you get all that bread?" asked Catfish.

"Hatfield there went to baker's school in the Army. All we do is bring along the flour and supplies and he sets up a portable oven every night and turns out a batch."

"Well, you fellas sure travel first class," Catfish said with admiration.

"Got to in this business," chuckled Mr. Plumbad. "The next town we come to we'll load up and be ready for another month of roughin' it. This stretch has been the worst. Once we get a little further south we'll be livin' civilized again."

When all had eaten their fill they helped themselves to the water keg. When it came Jib's turn he raised the dipper to his mouth but stopped to stare into it.

"Gosh! This water's alive!"

Without looking up, Mr. Hatfield said, "Crawlikins."

"Crawlikins?" asked Jib.

"Little creatures what swims in streams," explained Mr. Plumbad. "Been drinking 'em down for years. Never hurt me none. Never hurt the rest of us none neither. Fact is, we kinda got to likin' 'em."

Jib's Adam's apple did a dance. He quickly passed the dipper on.

That afternoon the sun came out for the first time since the storm. And with it the crew of the *Albatross* felt their spirits rise. It was agreed that the thing to do was to see what kind of shape the *Albatross* was in. And since everyone couldn't make the trip down the creek at the same time, Catfish took the two boys and Mr. Plumbad down first. Then Shandy returned and picked up the rest of the surveying crew. In half an hour they were all standing on the sandbar, shading their eyes and looking out at the houseboat. Mr. Plumbad said that from the way she was sitting she might have opened her seams along the starboard side.

"That's what we've got to find out," said Catfish. "The tide's on the ebb now, what say we go out and give it a look?"

Mr. Plumbad said, "Ahah," and the rest helped push them and the skiff through the surf until Catfish got the outboard started and they were on their way.

They circled the houseboat twice slowly, then stopped while Catfish climbed aboard and looked her over from stem to stern.

When the skiff brought them ashore again, the boys could tell that Catfish was elated over what he had seen.

"It's not bad at all," he yelled to them even before the skiff touched shore. "She's just sitting out there wedged in the mud. There's a couple feet of water in the cabin and part of the hold's flooded, but that's all."

"And that isn't bad?" asked Jib.

"Not near bad as it could be," grinned Catfish. "At least the engine's dry. What'd you think about it, Mr. Plumbad?"

The surveyor squinted at the houseboat over his glasses. "I think we should be able to figure out something. What this needs is a touch of scientific engineerin'. In other words, common sense."

"The first thing that needs doing is to get her bailed out. The bilge pump will take care of that in short order. But we got to figure out how to get her loose from that bar."

"Maybe we can use the outboard on the skiff to swing her free. Do you have a rope?" asked Mr. Plumbad.

"Plenty of it on board. We'd have to do it on a full tide though; she's sitting flat on the bottom now."

"Maybe you could crank up the houseboat's engine for a booster," said Yank.

"That's what I was thinkin'," put in Mr. Plumbad hastily. "If the outboard could do the pullin' and the engine gets the propeller turning, she might chew her way out."

"That's it," said Catfish. He glanced down the beach to see how far the water was from the high-tide mark. "She should be good and full toward the end of the afternoon. We'd better get that bilge pump to working right now."

"Right," said Plumbad. "Let's ferry everybody out to the boat. They can all help with the bailing or whatever else has to be fixed up."

Two trips of the skiff later, everyone was aboard the sloping deck of the *Albatross*, checking it over for damage. Two of the surveyors helped Catfish unlimber the boat's auxiliary bilge pump. They carried it aft and lashed it on a slant against the larboard scuppers just barely clear of the water. The hose was fed into the cabin through a porthole. For a while it looked as if the gasoline engine wasn't going to start, but finally, after a dozen pulls on the flywheel, it coughed and wheezed into life with a clanky popping sound that gradually quieted when the gurgling swish of water jetted out of the pump and over the side.

Once the cabin was pumped dry, the intake hose was shifted to the engine compartment and into the hold. When the boys saw the soggy shambles that had been left inside the cabin it was almost more than they could take. All of the bedding, their clothes, pots and pans and food from the galley, charts, books—everything movable was heaped in one unbelievable mess, all mixed up and covered with a sticky white paste that had once been dry flour.

They were the first ones to climb in and start pulling things apart, passing what was worth salvaging to some of the surveyors on deck for rinsing over the side. The bedding and clothes were tossed onto the wheelhouse or spread over the roof of the cabin for the sun to dry. After a while everyone was inside, scooping the worst out the portholes and using buckets of fresh salt water and a mop to clear away the rest.

It was a slow job but by late afternoon the cabin could be considered almost livable again and the bilge pump was gulping up air with the last few inches of water remaining in the hold.

On deck Catfish shut off the engine and coiled up the hose. Yank and Bill Zeffer carried it forward and stowed it in the wheelhouse.

"The tide's near about full," Catfish told Mr. Plumbad. "We might as well take everyone ashore, then give it a try with the skiff."

"Ahah," nodded Mr. Plumbad. "I'll handle the little boat. Had some experience with this sort of thing when a barge ran aground in the Mississippi River once."

Catfish refueled the outboard, then carried the others in to the beach.

Everyone watched from shore as the skiff returned to the *Albatross* and Mr. Plumbad exchanged places with Catfish. The captain brought out a coil of rope and attached one end to the stern of the skiff. The other end was made fast to the bow of the houseboat. Mr. Plumbad started the outboard and slowly moved out into deeper water. Catfish stuck his head out of the wheelhouse to yell something to him, then the rope tightened and swung up, dripping, out of the water.

At the same time those on shore heard the grinding hum of the starter coaxing the *Albatross*' engine. It ground over and over, but nothing happened. Shandy gritted his teeth, and Jib clenched his fists until his fingernails were hurting his palms.

The starter went: *Uhhhoooogahhhooooooogah . . . ah . . . ah . . . uhhhooogah . . .* , then at last the engine: *ah . . .*

*CHUNK . . . ahCHUNK . . . aCHUNK . . . aCHUNKa
. . . CHUNKaCHUNKaCHUNKaCHUNKa-CHUNK-
CHUNK-CHUNK-CHUNK.* A cheer went up from the watchers on shore.

Then all of a sudden the engine groaned and stopped.

Catfish came out on deck and waved the skiff in. The boys saw him coiling the rope. He looked over the stern, then he climbed into the skiff with Mr. Plumbad and they came ashore.

"What happened, Captain?"

"Busted her pin and spun the prop clean off."

"Gee whiz," groaned Jib.

Yank hooked his thumbs in his hip pockets. "You'll need a diver to get her fixed now."

He had hardly gotten the words out of his mouth when Shandy grabbed Jib's arm. "Did you hear what he just said?"

The boy's eyes brightened. "Yeah! Why not!"

"What's that?" asked Catfish.

"Why couldn't Jib and I fix it using our scuba gear?"

For three seconds no one said anything, then everyone talked at once.

"By golly!" Catfish exclaimed. "It might work!"

"Scuba's the answer all right," said Yank.

"You don't reckon the prop's busted a blade, do you?" asked Mr. Plumbad.

"No matter if it did, we got a spare one," said Catfish. "But if it didn't," he frowned, "it'll still be a trick finding the nut in all that mud."

"If it's there we'll find it," said Shandy.

"Listen," interrupted Mr. Plumbad. "Let one of my men handle this diving thing. These boys are too young for that."

"Don't worry about them," said Catfish. "They were taking YMCA lessons on how to handle scuba almost as soon as they learned how to swim. They may be young but they probably know more about diving than the whole bunch of us put together."

"All right" said Mr. Plumbad. "You just tell us how we can help."

"The lungs are aboard the *Albatross*," said Shandy. "What else do we need, Catfish?"

"Once you find the nut I don't think you'll need more than a pair of pliers and a cotter pin. That won't be any problem. What we really need, though, is to have some of that mud dug out from around the stern and maybe along the starboard side so it won't happen again. Think you boys could manage anything like that?"

"We'll try!" they both answered eagerly.

Catfish turned to Mr. Plumbad. "Do you fellas have anything to dig with?"

"A posthole digger and a couple of short-handled spades we use for digging out the truck if we get stuck."

"Good. I can run one of your men up the creek and we'll get them." Catfish started for the skiff, then stopped and turned around. "I just happened to think. If we get her loose we still got another problem. There's no anchor on her. We lost everything we had in the storm."

"We can fix you up in that department too," said Mr. Plumbad cheerfully. He called to his stake setter, Hatfield.

"Bring down about four of them concrete bench markers and any rope you can find. Yank, you go along with them and cut two or three pines about as thick as your arm and long enough to prize with."

The men nodded and dragged the skiff over the bar into the creek. Catfish cranked up the outboard and they soon disappeared into the sawgrass.

Moonrakers'
Luck

IT WASN'T LONG before the captain and the men were back with the shovels, poles, ropes, and four heavy concrete posts Mr. Plumbad explained were for burying in the ground to mark certain surveyor's points on their line.

Catfish and the boys made the trip back to the houseboat and unloaded the skiff. Shandy and Jib quickly put on their swimming suits and got out their diving lungs from the storage compartments while Catfish went ashore for Mr. Plumbad and two other men from the surveying crew.

By the time he came back the boys had checked over their gear and were ready to dive. Catfish got his toolbox from the wheelhouse and set it on the deck near the stern. "Here's all you'll need." He handed Shandy a pair of pliers and a metal pin. "First you've got to find the prop, then the large nut that screws on after the prop is put on the shaft. The cotter pin goes through a hole in the nut, just like on an outboard motor. Be sure you spread it out with the pliers on the other side."

The boys nodded.

"If the prop's damaged in any way—say a blade's bent or missing—put it on anyway. I don't want to use the good one unless we have to."

"All right," said Shandy. He spit on the glass of his face mask and rinsed it off so that it wouldn't fog underwater. Then he put it on, shoved the mouthpiece into his mouth, and inhaled. The cool compressed air filled his lungs. He gave a thumbs-down signal to Jib, pressed his mask tightly against his face, and slid off the stern into the water.

In a cloud of bubbles his weight belt carried him the short distance to the bottom. Glancing up, he saw Jib drifting down beside him. The bottom was soft and oozy. Mud that had been stirred up by starting the engine made the visibility bad. But in front of them was the dim gray outline of the hull. They moved close to it and began feeling with their feet. Shandy reached down and slipped off his rubber swim fins so that his feet would sink deeper in the mud. Sinking well over his ankles, he wiggled his toes, then shuffled sideways and tried it again. He felt nothing and he realized that all he was doing was stirring up the mud so they wouldn't be able to see anything.

Finally Shandy settled flat on his stomach and slowly worked his arms through the ooze under the stern. It was several minutes before his fingers touched something hard and metallic. Then he felt a blade. Gradually he got his fingers, then his hands around it and worked it free of the mud. The propeller didn't feel damaged. Jib was beside him with his arms up to his elbows in the mud. Shandy tapped him on his shoulder and pressed the propeller against him to let him know he had found it. Then he moved back and with one kick he shot to the surface, spit out his mouthpiece, and held the propeller up to the captain.

"By golly, you found it!" said Catfish.

"I think it's all right too," gasped Shandy. "Give me one of the shovels—we'll have to move some mud to get in to the shaft."

"All right. Be careful now." As he passed down a shovel Jib broke the surface, grinning broadly, with the big nut clenched in his fist.

"Good work," shouted Catfish. "Now if you can get some of that bottom cleared away maybe she'll run free when we put her together."

Back on the bottom the boys went to work with the shovels, scooping away the mud under the hull until they had made a three-foot-deep hole that completely cleared the stern and the shaft where the propeller would be attached. It was easy work but they did it by touch in the dark, the mud swirling around them until it was impossible to see even the outline of the hull when it was a foot in front of them. In an hour they surfaced only once, for spare air tanks, then they finished clearing a sizable trench from the stern to the bow along the starboard side of the houseboat.

As soon as the mud settled again, Shandy took the propeller and nut down and screwed them on the drive shaft exactly as Catfish had instructed. Then he inserted the pin, bent back the protruding ends, and surfaced.

"She's all set," he said as the others hauled him aboard. Hatfield and Yank had spaced the three pine poles along the port side, and the boys slipped off their diving gear and grabbed hold of the third pole to help prize.

This time the rope from the skiff was attached to the houseboat's stern.

"All right!" Catfish signaled to Mr. Plumbad. The outboard cranked up and the rope swung taut out of water. The captain pushed the starter and the *Albatross'* engine chugged into action. The whole boat vibrated. Then he put it in reverse. Mud, water, and sand boiled up around the stern and amidship. He slowly advanced the throttle. "Push!" he yelled.

Everyone leaned hard on the poles. The rope to the skiff sagged, then twanged tight and vibrated. The *Albatross* began shaking and groaning with the effort. Muddy water heaved and frothed around the boat, then there was a grinding crunch of the hull against the bottom. At first it started slowly, humping to break free of the sucking mud, then it grew louder into one long hull-hissing slide backward. She was free!

A tremendous cheer went up from everyone aboard. Yank untied the skiff line and Mr. Plumbad coiled it. Catfish backed the *Albatross* well out into deep water, threw her into forward gear, and nosed her bow out into the Gulf. He made a wide circle that brought them alongside the skiff, and Mr. Plumbad climbed aboard and tied the boat to the railing. "Well," he said, grinning broadly, "I reckon she's as good as she ever was, ain't she?" The safety pins down the front of his shirt stretched themselves to their utmost.

"I can't thank y'all enough," said Catfish, sincerely grateful. "We couldn't have done it alone."

"Aw, stuff," snorted Mr. Plumbad modestly. "It's them boys done all the work."

"They sure did," agreed Yank, with Hatfield adding a solemn nod.

The captain beamed at them. "I'd just as soon not think where we'd been if it hadn't been for you two with your diving gear, and that's the truth."

Shandy and Jib both began feeling uneasy with the attention they were getting and they lost no time hurrying aft to get their equipment stowed away.

Chuckling happily to himself, Catfish steered the *Albatross* as close to shore as he dared, then the men tied ropes around the cement posts and threw them over. They settled to the bottom and buried themselves in the mud, anchoring the boat securely.

It was a tired but happy crew that came ashore in the skiff, and it was an even happier group that greeted them.

"Seems this calls for the best blamed celebration supper a crew of castaways could cook up," grinned Catfish. He reached into the skiff and hoisted a bulging duffel bag Shandy had seen him put in just before they left the houseboat. "How long's it been since y'all had any canned ham, canned yams, canned collards, and a side order of fresh-netted mullet?"

"Now you're talkin' my language," said Mr. Plumbad, beaming over the top of his glasses.

At dusk, under the great cypress with the fire snapping sparks into the calm warm air, they feasted like hungry men who hadn't seen food for a month. In fact, they ate up a week's supply. Afterward Mr. Plumbad staggered to his feet and made a short speech, thanking them "for the best blamed rations this crew's had since last Thanksgivin'." Then he sat down and the men settled back with their pipes while Catfish told them the whole story about the old telescope with the pirate map on it and how they were going to try to find the treasure if Mr. Scanlon and the *Raven* didn't stop them.

"This Scanlon fella sounds like a real snake in the grass to try an' get what's rightfully Shandy's and his aunt's," said Mr. Plumbad, looking sternly over his spectacles. "What's your plans now?"

"Seein' how the *Albatross* is shipshape again, I guess our best bet is to shove off tonight and make it to the Steinhatchee River for supplies, then on down the coast."

The boys perked up their ears.

"Sure wish we could help you get away from that Scanlon fella," Mr. Plumbad said, wagging his head. "With that big cruiser of his he could run you down anywhere he pleased out there and nobody'd be the wiser. Fact is, it's a wonder he didn't find ya here and do ya in."

"That's why we didn't dare light any signal fires at night," said Jib. "We were afraid he might see them."

Mr. Plumbad put a finger alongside his nose, and his eyes in the firelight looked as if they were drawing up into tiny black dots behind his spectacles. He was smiling, almost.

"I got an idea," he said slowly, "a regular ripsnorter."

Everybody leaned forward because Mr. Plumbad started talking in a low voice that fairly charged the air with tension.

"Y'all know what a moonraker is?" he asked.

Everyone shook his head, even Yank.

"He's a gent that rakes up his profits when the moon ain't out," said Mr. Plumbad, going on to explain. "Years ago when there weren't no lighthouses and all the boats were sailing ships loaded with real fancy cargo, these gents I'm talkin' about used to set fires on the beach to guide ships into safe harbors. Only they weren't safe harbors, they were reefs. And when a ship ran aground they just went out and stole everything they could carry away. That's how they come by the name of moonrakers, see?"

"But how's that going to help these fellows?" asked Yank.

Mr. Plumbad held up his hand for silence. "What if we was to set some fires along the beach after y'all got away and see if we could trick them into thinkin' it was y'all here on the beach?"

"It sounds fine," said Catfish, "except for one thing. They aren't gonna let themselves run aground."

"They don't need to," said Mr. Plumbad. "All they gotta do is put over a boat and come ashore to see. Leave the rest of it to us." He chuckled deep in his throat and looked over the top of his spectacles at the other men in his crew. None of them said anything but they all grinned back at him. And the short one called Bill Zeffer was flicking his thumb against the edge of his machete as if he were just itching to use it. A shiver of excitement ran down Shandy's back.

"It might work at that," said the captain. "Leastways it'd give us a chance to get a head start."

With the whole crew working to help them, Catfish and the boys loaded all their gear aboard the *Albatross,* checked their fuel to make sure they had enough to reach their next destination, and went through the sad business of saying good-by. Shandy, for one, felt bad about leaving their new friends behind in the lonely swamp. But on the deck of the *Albatross,* Mr. Plumbad was all smiles when they shook his hand for the last time.

"No need to worry none about us," he said, looking at them over his glasses. "We're creatures of the woods, you know. Maybe one day when we get our topo line hacked out we might run into y'all again, who knows?" He cocked his head. "Ahah . . . Well, good-by. Take care of yourselves now. We'll keep the home fires burning," and off he went with a wave as Catfish took him ashore in the skiff.

It was almost an hour later that Mr. Plumbad leaned down and touched a match to the first pile of firewood on the bar. Shortly afterward another blazed up a short distance away, then a third.

"Do ya think they can see 'em from the houseboat?" asked Bill Zeffer.

"Sure they can," said Mr. Plumbad. "Now all we gotta do is keep 'em burnin' big and bright, and see what us moonrakers can rake in tonight."

"Doggonit, if you ain't a poet," muttered the little man.

It was close to midnight when Mr. Plumbad touched his companion's shoulder and gently awakened him.

"What's up, chief?"

"Ahah, look yonder," whispered Mr. Plumbad. "Appears we got us some visitors." He nodded toward the moon-swept Gulf where a large yacht was anchored. A dinghy with three figures in it was being rowed ashore.

As it grounded on the sand bar, Mr. Plumbad stepped forward to meet them.

"Howdy," he said. "Whatch'all doin' out this time a night?"

The three men said nothing, but they climbed out of the boat and walked toward the two surveyors and the fire. One of them was a hulk of a man, towering over the others. He kept glancing beyond the fires into the darkness and blinking. The other man stayed back a little with his hand in his jacket pocket. The third was Mr. Scanlon.

"What are you doing here with the fires?" he asked sharply.

"Some friends of ours are due in tonight from Saint Marks," said Mr. Plumbad. "They're in a houseboat and we was afraid they couldn't find their way ashore unless we put up a marker for 'em."

"Two boys and an old man?"

"Sure, that's them—how'd you know, stranger? They friends of yours?"

"Why, yes," Mr. Scanlon said. "They're good friends of ours." His manner was suddenly more friendly. He walked over and looked down at the fire. "What are they doing here, though?" he asked.

"Beats me," said Mr. Plumbad. Then he explained how his surveying crew met them. But he didn't tell him that the boys and the captain had been castaways and that the *Albatross* had run aground in the storm.

"They shoved off for Saint Marks for more supplies," he added, with a healthy stretch of the truth.

"You say they had a camp up at the head of the creek and were cutting away vines in a clearing above it?" Mr. Scanlon's eyes glittered in the firelight.

"That they did," said Mr. Plumbad. "I got the feelin' they were lookin' for somethin'."

Mr. Scanlon glanced at him sharply.

"Just take your dinghy and follow that creek there," said Mr. Plumbad. "It'll take you to their camp. The rest of my crew is up there. You can't miss it."

"Well, we might just do that," said Mr. Scanlon. "I'd like to see what my friends have been up to for the last couple days." Then over his shoulder he barked an order to the other men.

"Drag the boat over the bar. We're going up the creek."

When Mr. Plumbad was certain they had done just that, he turned to his instrument man.

"Zeffer, how are you at swimmin'?"

"I wouldn't drown if that's whatcha mean."

"Well, start peelin' off. We got a little job to do out yonder." Mr. Plumbad was looking over his spectacles toward the black silhouette of the *Raven*.

Ten minutes later they pulled themselves, grunting and sputtering, up the cruiser's Jacob's ladder and into the cockpit. Mr. Plumbad fumbled around in the darkness until his hand touched a length of heavy manila rope. He handed it to his shivering companion.

"Here, get over the side and wrap this around the props good and tight."

"Right." The little man climbed down the ladder and disappeared with the rope.

Mr. Plumbad felt along the corner of the stern until he found and unscrewed the cap to the cruiser's fuel tanks. Then he went down the ladder into the water again. Holding his nose, he upended and kicked furiously for the bottom. When he gurgled to the surface a few seconds later he was clutching a handful of mud and sand. With more grunting and sputtering he hoisted himself high out of the water and deposited the gritty mass through the fuel tank opening into the stomach of the powerful diesels. With a chuckle he screwed the cap back in place, then hauled his winded instrument man back up the Jacob's ladder.

"You all right, Zeffer?"

"F-f-fine, I r-r-reckon," stammered his companion, "seein' I s-swallered only half the Gulf."

"Good," said Mr. Plumbad, dropping to his knees and sweeping his hands across the deck just back of the helm.

"Wh-whatja lose?"

"Nothin'. Gotta find . . ." He found the tiny latch and lifted it. "Give me a hand, now."

Together they slid open the hatch cover of the engine compartment. "C'mon," said Mr. Plumbad. He scrambled down into the pitch-black hole with Zeffer right behind him.

"What do we do now?" whispered the instrument man.

"Just grab and pull loose every wire you can lay your hands on. An' if you can get anything else off these blasted diesels, throw it over the side."

In no time the two of them were so caught up in the damage they were doing to the cruiser's great engines that they failed to hear the dinghy as it bumped against the Jacob's ladder. But they did hear the heavy footfalls as a man jumped aboard and came across the deck.

"What we gonna—?"

"Sh-h-h-h!" Mr. Plumbad's hand closed on a monkey wrench he had found in the darkness. Cautiously he crawled back to the hatch and peeked out. A shadowy figure was bent over something near the bulkhead. Mr. Plumbad eased out of the engine compartment. Soundlessly he crept across the deck and raised the wrench over the man just as he turned.

"Hey!" the man shouted.

"Yank! You idiot, I almost brained ya. Whatcha doin' here?"

"The same thing you fellas are, I guess."

"Where's Scanlon and his two apes?"

"We took 'em out to show 'em where the vines were cut, just like you wanted. They took our shovels and the last time I saw 'em they were digging mud holes all over the place. I borrowed their dinghy to come get you."

"Good thinkin'," chuckled Mr. Plumbad. "The rest of the crew still in camp?"

"Right. They're waiting on us."

"Then I reckon this is all we can do here. Let's go."

Not long afterward they were rowing up the creek toward the big cypress. "While our guests are diggin' for treasure we'll just melt back up the line and fade away for a spell. Maybe go back and measure the line with Lucas and Scuffmore for a couple days." A look of genuine contentment came over Mr. Plumbad's face. Suddenly it changed to remorse.

"The radio, dadblameit! We forgot their radio!"

Yank reached in his pocket and held up something that gleamed in the moonlight. It was a radio tube.

Mr. Plumbad settled his arm affectionately on the Yank's shoulder.

"You stick with me, son, and I'll make you the best doggone surveyor the gov'ment ever had, even if you are a Yankee."

The
Great
Spring

LATE the next night the captain stuck his head out the wheelhouse window of the *Albatross* and asked the boys to watch for a flashing green beacon. They picked out the light long before they reached it, then they spotted another farther to the left. They passed both on their port side.

It wasn't long afterward that they saw another flashing light beacon; when they reached this one they turned in and immediately began picking their way between a series of can buoys marking the channel into Crystal River.

What mystified the boys was that they could make out the low black shoreline but there wasn't a single sign of a town or a light of any kind. The closer they got the more puzzled they were, until finally they climbed down from the cabin roof and squeezed into the wheelhouse with Catfish.

"Are you sure this is the right place?" Jib asked anxiously.

"We can't see anything ahead of us but land. No buildings, nothing."

"That's right," Catfish chuckled in the darkness of the wheelhouse. All but the boat's running lights were shut off so he could see the channel markers better. "What we're going through now are called the Crystal Reefs," he explained. "They're a lot of shallow sand bars. What you see up ahead is about a thousand little mangrove islands, kinda like the pieces of a jigsaw puzzle all scrambled up. The channel takes us through them and into Crystal River. Then we got about four miles to go after that and we'll be in the best hideout port you ever saw. It's called Kings Bay."

"Gosh, I wish it was light enough so we could see it," said Jib.

"You'll see it tomorrow," Catfish promised. "This river's got some of the greatest tarpon fishing in Florida."

It was slow going up the river because there were occasional sand bars they had to be careful of. The black jagged outline of jungle growth on either side of them stood out sharply against the sky. Once in a while their passing frightened some huge bird roosting in the trees overhanging the water. Then there would be a startled squawk, a flapping of wings, and a thrashing of vegetation as the bird took to the air.

Finally the *Albatross* cleared the opening into Kings Bay. Ahead of them were the lights of a large hotel close to the water's edge. And farther to the left were more lights, but they were some distance away and made a bright glow in the sky. Catfish explained that they were the lights from the town of Crystal River.

They crossed the bay and drew up at a darkened wharf.

"We'll tie up here for the rest of the night," said Catfish. "Then, first thing in the morning, we'll see my friend at the Chamber of Commerce and make arrangements to have the boat looked over."

From the darkness across the bay came the booming grunt of an alligator.

"Boy," mumbled Jib, pricking up his ears. "Listen to that big bullfrog!"

The bay was only a short distance from Crystal River, the boys discovered the next morning when they caught a taxi at the hotel near the wharf and rode into town with Catfish. It was a small, clean-looking community with one-story buildings lining both sides of the main street. The taxi turned a corner and stopped in front of a building with big windows. In gold letters on the glass it said: West Citrus County Chamber of Commerce.

Inside, beneath a colored wall map at the far end of the room, a thick-shouldered white-haired man was bent over a pile of papers strewn on his desk. A stubby cigar was clenched firmly in the corner of his mouth and a cloud of bluish smoke hovered over his head like a threatening squall.

Abruptly he looked up. His jaw dropped open and his cigar almost fell out. "Catfish Jackson!" he roared, lurching halfway across his desk. "What in thunder brings you down here?"

"The stink of your infernal cigars," grinned the captain as the big man wrung his hand as if he were trying to unscrew it at the wrist. "How're ya doin', Major?"

"Great, just great! Say—you've put on a little weight since I saw you last."

"That's what comes from bein' retired," said Catfish. "I wantcha to meet my shipmates here." He introduced the boys, who shook hands with the major.

"Draw up a chair," said the major. "How long y'all plan to be with us?"

"Not long, I'm afraid," said Catfish. "A bad storm hit us up the coast and I figure we'd better have the houseboat looked over to see how much damage it did us."

"We can take care of that right away. But what's the rush? We got tarpon in. Why not stay and get in some fishing?"

"Nothin' we'd like better," said Catfish, "except that the boys and me got us a treasure to find."

The major's eyebrows went up. "Oh, you're on a treasure hunt? Well, they say the pirates left a lot of it somewhere around here. Trouble is," he added, "nobody's ever turned up a single doubloon."

"Accordin' to our map, this place is down around Tampa," said the captain.

"Tampa, huh. I used to live in a little town called Sun City just across the bay. It's grown up considerably since then, though."

"Did you ever know of a shell island around there?" asked Catfish.

The major shrugged. "Sure, plenty of them. We got a couple around here too."

"We figure this one's somewhere along the east side of the bay."

The major frowned and chewed his cigar thoughtfully. "There was one—big overgrown place called Mound Key. Here, let me show you on the map." He spun his chair around and stood up in front of the map behind his desk.

"There it is, right there." The major put his finger on the map. "Little place called Cockroach Bay. Mound Key is smack in the middle of it. A whole island of shells."

"Hey," said Shandy. "Remember that picture of a beetle on the map? Jib said it looked like a roach. D'ya suppose . . ."

"Island's covered with cockroaches," said the major. "Probably how the bay got its name."

"Then that's where we're headed soon as we can get the *Albatross* checked over," said Catfish.

"Can't say as I envy you," said the major, "but I'll give you all the help I can." He reached for the telephone. "I'll call Chet Barlow and have him pull out your boat right away. In the meantime you might take the boys over to the Bait House for a look at the springs. Once they get a gander at all those fish they might want to forget about going treasure hunting."

"Major," said Catfish with a grin, "I'll never figure out how the Marines get along without you."

When they reached the Bait House, a long white building built on pilings over the water, a tanned man wearing a green-visored fishing cap, a spotless T-shirt, and faded blue jeans waved them onto the dock. He had just finished hosing off the deck of a small glass-bottomed boat with a striped awning mounted over it, and the dock was slippery.

"Catfish Jackson?" he asked. "I'm Dave Freeman. The major called and said you'd be right over. Hope you don't mind waiting a spell. It's chow time for our bass and they get pretty mad if I don't feed them right on the dot."

The captain wondered if he had heard right. "You gotta feed *what?*"

"Come on out front." Mr. Freeman led the way along a narrow catwalk beside the building. At the end of the dock he pointed down into the crystal-clear water. "There they are," he said with a smile. "The hungriest, laziest fish you've ever seen."

Catfish and the boys couldn't believe their eyes. "Scuttle my skiff if they aren't lined up like a bunch of choirboys!" the captain exclaimed.

More than a dozen big black bass hovered expectantly in front of the dock, not under it. And all of them were pointed in, not out, as if they were waiting for something to happen.

Mr. Freeman chopped up some mullet and held a piece two feet over the water. One of the huskier largemouths pushed forward, then leaped up and into the air, plucking the tidbit from his hand without even touching his fingers.

"Well, I'll be—"

Mr. Freeman had another fish repeat the trick to show them that it hadn't been an accident. Then he tossed out several pieces of mullet, and the bass had them almost before they hit the water. There was a swirl, a flash of fins, and the food was gone.

"My wife feeds about thirty of them every morning," said the Bait House man.

"But where do they all come from?" asked Jib.

"From fishermen who don't know they've caught more than their limit until the end of the day," he told them. "They release the extras at the dock and the fish have gotten in the habit of waiting around for handouts."

"Boy, they sure are tame," said Jib.

Catfish shook his head in disbelief. "If I ever tell anybody about this they'll think I'm dotty. Who ever heard of black bass taking mullet anyway?"

Mr. Freeman threw the remaining morsels to the fish. "There are a lot more strange things about this river," he said. "Let's take a run out to the Great Spring and I'll show you what I mean."

The five-horse outboard on the stern of the glass-bottomed boat pushed them across the bay at a leisurely pace, slow enough for them to see the strange world in the unbelievably clear depths beneath them. There were immense boulders surrounded by long-bladed grass that moved in the water like wind-blown dunes of sea oats in the fall. Bluegills, bass, and catfish swam side by side with salt-water trout, striped sheepsheads, and mangrove snappers. The bottom grew nearer, as the thick masses of sun-gilt grass leaned against a strong current, then suddenly it dropped away and long shafts of light reached down through dazzling blue emptiness.

"Gosh, it's like a hole in the sky!" said Jib.

"We're coming to the spring now," said Mr. Freeman. "See the boil on the surface up ahead." Waves of water churned and eddied upward from the middle of the calm bay.

"Look!" cried Shandy, pointing through the glass. "There it is!"

Far beneath them, almost beyond reach of the shafts of sunlight, was the source of the turbulence. At one edge of a wide, saucer-shaped depression a great overhanging ledge marked the mouth of the spring.

"And look at all the fish!"

"You name them and they're here," said Mr. Freeman. "Salt-water and fresh-water fish, feeding and living together as if they never had an enemy in the world."

"But why?" asked Shandy. "Why do they all come to the spring?"

The Bait House man shrugged. "Indian legend says that the spring heals anyone or anything that's sick. Old-timers claim that there's an Indian good-luck sign carved on that ledge down there—it's supposed to look like a swastika turned backwards. Nobody knows how it got there; all I know is that those salt-water fish have come many a mile to get here."

"There's some tarpon," said Catfish as three fish well over five feet long came floating through the depths like three silver ghosts. They paused and hovered motionless in the currents that flowed upward around them. A swarm of smaller fish moved like a dense black cloud near the mouth of the spring while hundreds of sunfish flitted about with the lightness of butterflies. Big fish and little fish milled in gentle confusion while the giant spring poured out its endless torrents of water.

Feeling almost as if he were a part of this strange life in the blue void beneath him, Jib suddenly asked, "Have you ever seen any sea monsters in the spring?"

For a moment Mr. Freeman said nothing. Catfish, who had started to smile at the boy's question, glanced up.

"Well," said the Bait House man thoughtfully, "I guess you couldn't say there are any *real* sea monsters. But sometimes . . ." he paused, "sometimes you see things in the spring that you can't rightly explain. Of course I reckon anything that wanted to could come out of the sea and find its way here—even a real live sea monster," he said with a wink to the boys.

They circled the spring again, then Mr. Freeman rode them to the marina where the *Albatross* was being looked over. When they got there the houseboat was still in the water.

"The major said you were in a big hurry," Mr. Barlow told the captain, "so I hauled her out, put a little calking in a couple of seams, patched the hole in the foredeck, and slid her back in again. She's as good as she ever was."

"That's sure a relief," said Catfish. "How much do I owe you?"

"No charge," smiled the man. "Compliments of the Chamber of Commerce." He waved and walked off before Catfish had a chance to thank him.

The captain turned to the boys. "Well, by golly, then I reckon we can start makin' waves for Mound Key. We still got some piece to go."

Mysterious
Mound
Key

THEY TRAVELED all that day and that night, taking turns sleeping, and by midmorning of the following day they were approaching Tampa Bay. One big ocean liner after another passed the *Albatross,* heading out. Then they went up the shipping lanes into the bay and a little later passed under a tremendously long, high bridge. Far to the left were the buildings and marinas of St. Petersburg. But instead of turning in to that big city, they turned right in a direction where there was no city at all. As they drew closer, the boys realized that what they thought was land was really overgrown mangrove islands of all sizes and shapes, close together.

"Are you sure this is the right place?" Shandy asked Catfish. "All those islands look alike."

"We're coming to it," he said, keeping one eye on the chart and the other on the depth finder.

A few minutes later the islands thinned, the shoreline dipped in, and the *Albatross* lumbered into a shallow bay at quarter speed. Then the boys saw that one large island stood out from all the others. It was tall and steep, and as the *Albatross* came closer, Shandy glimpsed patches of white shells showing through the green undergrowth.

"That's it!" he shouted. "That's Mound Key—look at all the shells!"

Catfish quickly shut off the engine and the boys scurried forward to drop the anchor.

"Not much of a bay," said Catfish, "but bless my binnacle if the major wasn't right. Mound Key sticks up like a sore thumb smack in the middle of it."

"Can we go ashore right away?" asked Jib excitedly.

"Soon as we can get the skiff over the side and into the water," said Catfish.

The boys quickly unfastened it and flipped it over the lee rail on the side facing the island.

"Might be a good idea to take the scope with us," said Catfish.

In the cabin he unlocked the padlock of his sea chest, took out the old telescope, and held it up to the light where they could all see the strange but familiar inscriptions on the glowing brass surface.

"I sure hope there aren't any—" Shandy stopped short.

"What's wrong?" said Jib.

"Listen!"

A quiet throbbing hum came from outside.

"Just a boat going by," said Catfish. But Shandy was already across the cabin, looking out the porthole.

"It's *them*!" he whispered sharply. "It's the *Raven*!"

Catfish leaped to his side. "By golly, it is! And the varmints are putting over a dinghy!" He pushed the telescope into Shandy's hands. "Take it and get to the island quick. You got a couple of minutes yet. Keep the houseboat between you and the cruiser."

"But what about you?"

"Never mind me. It's the scope they're after. Now git!"

Keeping low, the boys ran along the starboard side of the houseboat and climbed down into the skiff. Shandy shoved them off with the sculling oar, then dropped it into its slot and sculled for the island as hard as he could go.

The skiff barely made it around a clump of mangroves when the dinghy pulled up to the stern of the houseboat. Mr. Scanlon and two other men climbed aboard.

"C'mon," whispered Jib. "Let's go before they come looking for us."

Shandy sculled the skiff along the far side of the island. Everywhere the mangroves were so thick that they made an almost impenetrable shield around the island. The branches thrust out from shore as if to ward off any intruders, and their strong slender roots reached down to anchor themselves in the channel bottom like bars in a fence.

"Gosh, I don't think we can get on the island," said Jib.

"I saw one place where we might make it," said Shandy. "There was a big banyan tree on the bank between the mangroves." He turned the skiff around and sculled back to the spot.

The light gray peeling bark of the banyan tree stood out sharply against the darker mangroves. Like the mangroves, the banyan ran roots down from its branches, but they were massive and sturdy like the trunk of the tree itself.

Jib took the oar and worked the skiff in close to the overhanging foliage while Shandy stood in the bow keeping a sharp lookout for sun-basking snakes on the branches. He caught hold of a smooth, well-arched banyan root and tied the boat to it.

Then he climbed up on it. "Come on," he said.

The bank was muddy from the high tide, so the boys climbed through the branches until they were over solid ground, then they slid down one of the roots.

They landed in a narrow, weed-choked thicket and were surprised to see a steep hill rising behind them. Big coils of finger-thick vines with inch-long thorns wove a solid barrier around it.

The top of the hill had to be the highest point on the island. "We could see all sides if we could get through those briers," said Shandy. "Let's take a look."

Paying particular attention to where they stepped and what they stepped on, the boys worked their way along the bottom until they found a tunnel-like opening just large enough for them to squeeze through on their stomachs.

"This'd be a lot easier if we—ouch!—had our machetes," moaned Jib, sticking close to Shandy's heels.

Once they cleared the entanglement they were able to stand up. Ahead of them was a gradually rising incline of shoulder-high grass dotted with short palm trees. It rose steeply to a rounded knoll.

They fought their way up the remaining few yards and reached the top puffing like locomotives.

"Gosh, who'd ever thought the island was this high? You can't even see Cockroach Bay or the *Albatross*!"

Jib was right. It looked as if they were standing on a hilltop overlooking a huge green pasture that stretched in all directions. Tampa Bay and St. Petersburg glittered in the distance, but there was no sign that this carpet of green was really islands with channels between them.

"Maybe that's why we couldn't see the hill from the water," said Shandy. "There were too many mangroves."

Jib walked to the edge of the knoll.

"You'd better watch where you're standing; that drops off pretty—hey, look!" Shandy started scraping the sand away from a white, rounded object near Jib's foot.

"What'd you find?"

Shandy pulled it out of the dirt. "Look, it's a conch shell —just like the picture on the scope!"

The boys stared at each other. Then both of them started digging. Two other large shells appeared. And beneath them there were fragments of others. The more they dug the more they found. In fact there were shells of one kind or another no matter where they broke through the thin layer of loose sandy dirt covering them. And each time they removed a shell, several large cockroaches scurried for cover.

"The whole island's shells, all right," said Shandy.

"And roaches," added Jib with a shiver.

"Right. That takes care of the pictures of the cockroach and the shell. But what could that black half moon, the skull, and those crossed swords mean?"

"I think the swords are an *X*. Treasure maps always

have an *X* on them someplace—that's where the treasure is."

Shandy scratched his head. "I don't know," he said. "Everything else fits in. It's gotta mean something more than 'this is the island' or 'this is the place.' " He studied the scope again but it still didn't make sense. He walked over to the spot where he had dug up the first shell and looked down the hill. It dropped off abruptly for several yards, then gradually sloped down to the mangroves.

"Let me see the picture again," said Jib.

Shandy handed him the scope.

There was nothing really different about the hill in any direction he looked at it. The north side was maybe a little steeper and more angular than the other sides but that was all. There were no big trees or significant rocks or an unusual landmark of any kind.

"Hey, Shandy, if this triangle means the island, you don't suppose this half moon in the center of it means they've buried the treasure right in the middle of the mound, do you?"

"I guess that makes more sense than anything else."

Jib frowned. "Gee, that'd be terrible. We'd never be able to dig it out from under all these shells—never in a million years!"

"Don't worry about that," Shandy said. "If a pirate was going to hide his treasure in the middle of a hill he'd find an easier way of doing it than by digging."

"I guess you're right," Jib agreed with relief. "If it was up to me I'd hunt me a cave or something."

Shandy glanced up. "What'd you say?"

"I said I'd hunt—"

"That's what the half moon is—a cave!"

"Yeah, come to think of it, the drawing looks just like the mouth of a cave! But where could it be?"

"Right here"—Shandy poked his finger at the triangle —"halfway down the side of the hill."

"But which side?"

Shandy's seemingly sound guesswork suddenly lost its importance when he realized that if there was a cave it would surely be hidden. And without knowing where to look, it would be like trying to find a needle in a haystack.

"Gosh, you'd think those pirates would have had enough sense to put better directions on their map," he said in disgust. "Here they went and put a compass rose on it to show how to get here but nothing on the island to show which way to look for the treasure."

"Maybe that's the secret," said Jib. He looked at the map again. "Say-y-y Shandy, that could be it. The corners of the triangle are pointing exactly north, east, and west. But the crossed swords are over the corner pointing north!"

"Halfway down the north side of the island! It's worth a try. Let's go!"

They started down the steep incline, slipping and sliding on the exposed surfaces of shells. Jib, who was ahead, broke into a run. Before he could check himself his legs were windmilling under him faster than he intended them to. The big patch of briers was right in his path when he purposely fell and rolled the rest of the way down to the edge of them before coming to a stop.

Feeling foolish, he got to his feet and dusted himself off. He looked back for Shandy and Shandy wasn't there!

It didn't make sense. Shandy had been right behind him.

He called. There was no answer. Jib started back up the hill.

He didn't have to go far before he saw the gaping hole in the ground half hidden by the tall grass. It looked as if it had caved in. As he lay down on his stomach and inched up to the edge of the hole, he was almost too scared to look in.

When he did, his eyes widened and he broke into a cold sweat.

Sprawled at the bottom of the deep dark pit, half covered with sand and broken shells, Shandy lay where he had fallen. Less than four feet in front of him, coiled and ready to strike, was the biggest rattlesnake Jib had ever seen.

Back to
Kings Bay

JIB CLENCHED his fists helplessly. He didn't know what to do. Shandy didn't move. He was facing the snake but Jib couldn't tell if he was unconscious or not. Several loose shells and dirt broke off from the brink and showered into the hole. The snake struck at them wildly.

Then Jib heard Shandy's voice. His lips hardly moved, he spoke so softly.

"Don't scare him, Jib."

Jib glanced around for some kind of weapon. There was nothing, and the hole was at least eight or ten feet deep.

The rattlesnake moved its ugly, fist-sized head. Its tongue darted in and out as it tried to sense the direction of the intruder. Shandy's stillness had protected him from discovery—so far. But the snake's rattles kept up a steady warning buzz like seeds rattling in a small gourd.

"W-what can I do?" Jib whispered.

"Sh-h-h-h," Shandy warned.

The snake slowly coiled and uncoiled as if inviting an attack. Its huge black-and-yellow diamondback body was as big around as a man's leg. Then suddenly the rattling ceased, the coils unwound, and the heart-shaped head moved forward. Cautiously the snake undulated through the shells and debris toward Shandy. It reached his foot, paused, then glided slowly alongside one of Shandy's legs.

Cold chills ran down Jib's back. He bit his lip so hard the iron taste of blood came to his mouth.

The rattlesnake crawled the entire length of Shandy's body until it reached one of his outstretched arms. Then it hesitated again, darting its tongue rapidly. Jib's heart stood still. Sandy's face was an ashen mask. Rivulets of sweat trickled slowly through the dust on his cheeks.

Apparently satisfied that the way was clear, the snake slithered over Shandy's arm, dragging its entire six-foot-long body across him in agonizingly slow motion. Then it disappeared from sight.

Shandy still lay as quiet as his surroundings, as if he were part of the shells and sand that covered him.

Neither of them spoke for a full three minutes, then Jib saw Shandy slowly turn his head toward the direction the snake had taken.

Nothing happened. He moved his arm, then braced his elbow against the ground and pushed himself up into a sitting position.

"Is he gone?"

"I think so. There's an opening between some big rocks behind me. He must have gone into it."

"Gosh, be careful. There may be another one around."

Shandy crawled painfully to his feet.

"How could you stand him that close to you without moving?"

Shandy wiped the sweat and grime off his face. "I couldn't move or he'd have found me. Didn't you see his eyes? They were pure white—he was blind."

"Oh my gosh!" Jib reached down as far as he could stretch. "Here, give me your hand and I'll pull you out."

"Okay." Looking around for something to stand on, Shandy saw something at his feet. "Wait a minute," he said.

He bent and picked up a long, yellowish, curved object.

"What's that?"

"It's a bone—a rib bone, I think." Then for the first time he looked around him. "Hey, Jib—there's old bones lying all over down here!"

"You don't suppose it's an old Indian burial mound, do you?"

"I don't know . . ." Shandy carefully pushed aside a mass of hairlike roots that almost concealed the roof of the pit. "It's part of a cave!" he exclaimed.

"Are you sure?"

"Positive. I can see some of those icicle-shaped things hanging down near the hole."

"Gosh, how far back does it go? Do you see a chest anywhere?"

Shandy examined the vault more closely. "No. As far as

I can tell, this is it. Both ends are caved in—must have happened a long time ago from the looks of it."

Using the piece of bone as a probe, Shandy cautiously moved some of the dangling clusters of roots that obscured the wall.

"The sides are all solid limestone," he called up. "I don't think—Hold it, here's something!"

"What is it?"

Shandy was silent for a few seconds. "It's a drawing . . . a kind of picture scratched real deep into the wall. It looks like an Indian good-luck sign—no, there's something else." He brushed away the dirt with his hand.

From above, Jib heard Shandy's startled exclamation. Then, "Pull me up, Jib! Get me out of here, quick!"

Jib reached down and they locked their hands around each other's wrists. With Shandy digging his toes in wherever he could and Jib pulling for all he was worth, Shandy finally made it out of the cave.

"Whew! Am I glad to be out of there." Shandy's face was covered with small scratches and there was a large bump on the side of his forehead. Jib pumped questions at him.

Shandy climbed to his feet and scuffed out a small flat clearing. "Remember what that man at Crystal River said about there being an Indian good-luck sign on the rock over the big spring?"

"Sure."

"Well, that was the first thing I saw scratched on the wall of the cave. Under it were some wavy lines." Shandy picked up a stick and marked the two pictures in the sand.

"I thought they were Indian pictures. But then right above these two there was a picture of two crossed swords, so the whole thing looked like this:"

Jib stared wide-eyed at the drawing. "Indians didn't have swords."

"Right. Those pictures were put there by the pirates. For some reason they moved the treasure out of this cave and I'll bet you anything it's somewhere around that spring at Crystal River!"

Jib jumped up eagerly. "We gotta get Catfish."

"Sure," said Shandy. "And now we got something to get him with. We don't need the scope any more. We'll use it to ransom him!"

"Swell idea, Shandy. C'mon, let's get back to the boat."

He led the way back down the hill through the tall grass to the heavy brier entanglement. There was no time to waste, and when they came out the other side they were both badly scratched. At the edge of the beach they picked their way through the mangroves until they reached the banyan tree where they had tied their boat. Quickly they climbed into the branches of the tree and dropped down into the skiff.

When they sculled out from behind the island they saw the *Raven*'s dinghy still tied to the stern of the *Albatross*. No one was on deck.

But as the skiff slid up beside the houseboat the cabin door was jerked open and Mr. Scanlon scowled at them.

"Well, well, look what we have here. I figured if you boys didn't get lost in the islands you'd have to come back here sooner or later. Get inside and be fast about it."

At the cabin door Jib gasped. It looked as if a hurricane had turned everything upside down. Their gear was dumped in the middle of the deck, drawers were open and emptied, the bunks were torn up, one of the lockers had even been ripped away from the bulkhead and dropped on its side. And Catfish was tied to a chair with his arms behind his back. Sitting opposite him was a big man in a baggy pair of brown shorts and a sports shirt with pictures of purple monkeys and orange palm trees on it. He had a black eye and he held a gun.

"Catfish, did they hurt you?" Jib started for the captain.

The big man jumped up. "Git back," he growled. "Both of you."

"I'm okay," Catfish reassured them. "Just wish I could get my hands on these varmints once more," he said through clenched teeth.

"Shut up!" hissed the fat man, gingerly touching his swollen cheek with a pudgy finger. "I've had about enough out of you."

"Take it easy, Blinky," said a man Shandy hadn't seen at first, coming away from the bulkhead behind them. He wore a black sweatshirt, a windbreaker, and khaki pants. "Pops here don't want no more trouble, do you, Pops?"

Catfish growled under his breath.

"Turk's right." Mr. Scanlon turned and glowered at the boys. "You two can save us *all* a lot of trouble," he said. "Just tell us where the telescope is."

"It's not your scope," Shandy burst out. "It belongs to my Uncle Martin!"

"But your Aunt Tilou sold me all his things," said Mr. Scanlon evenly. "Now by rights it belongs to me. Where've you hidden it?"

Shandy looked at Catfish, then back to Mr. Scanlon.

"Would you let us all go if I gave it to you?" he said suddenly.

Mr. Scanlon mellowed instantly. "Why certainly we would; that's all we want." He smiled warmly.

"Don't give 'em anything," said Catfish. "Specially the scope!"

"I'm not gonna tell ya again," grunted the big man, pushing his automatic under Catfish's nose.

"You all can go free and be on your way," repeated Mr. Scanlon. "I give you my word."

"Hmmmmph," muttered Catfish.

"In fact," added Mr. Scanlon quickly, "to show you how generous I am, if you give us the scope and we find the treasure, I'll personally see to it that your aunt—Martin's poor widow—gets a nice little share of it, how's that?"

"Don't listen to—"

"I'll do it!" exclaimed Shandy. He pulled the scope out of his shirt and handed it to Mr. Scanlon.

Catfish groaned.

Mr. Scanlon's smile froze on his lips. "You're clever," he said slowly. "I should have known you had it on you all the time."

"You mean we done all the work of tearin' up this

crumby joint for nothin'?" complained the fat man, wiping his sweaty face and jamming his automatic back under his shirt.

"Whatdaya plan to do with them now?" asked Turk.

"Do?" Mr. Scanlon turned the scope over slowly in his hands. "I'll do just as I said. I'll keep my word." His fingers gently stroked the figures etched on the dull brass surface. "I'm willing to let bygones be bygones." He smiled good-naturedly, and Shandy could tell that he was working up to something. Finally Mr. Scanlon said:

"I'll even go one better . . ." he paused. "I'll make a fair business deal with you. You tell me what you think these little pictures around this triangle mean, and I'll see that you get half the treasure." His head jerked nervously.

Shandy knitted his brows as if in deep thought. Finally he looked up with a friendly smile on his face. "It's a deal," he said.

Catfish's jaw dropped and Jib was so surprised he almost choked.

"Let me take the scope." Shandy reached out eagerly.

Mr. Scanlon hesitated a moment, then passed it over.

"Now the way I see it," said Shandy, "this place is on the east side of the bay because there's the compass rose showing the directions."

"Yes, yes, we know that," said Mr. Scanlon impatiently. "Go on."

"Well, ah . . . it's an island—a *mangrove* island off-shore."

"How do you know that?"

"Because the pictures are drawn outside the line that marks the bay."

"They are?" Mr. Scanlon leaned forward and stared at the inscription with renewed interest. "Yes-s-s, they *are,* aren't they. That's fine! What else do you see?"

"Well now . . ." Shandy frowned and turned the scope so that the light hit it better. "This triangle here is a three-sided—ah, clearing. That's it, and there's a big tree at each corner! Now that leaves just four pictures—a skull, a beetle, a coil of string, and crossed swords."

"That's right!" exclaimed Mr. Scanlon as it all became meaningful to him now.

Shandy's voice rose as he warmed to the tale and began talking faster and faster, "—and if that should turn out to be a *gold* beetle and the skull just happens to be in the tree marked with an *X* by the crossed swords, then we tie the beetle to the string and—"

"Yes, yes!" cried Mr. Scanlon, not remembering why he knew it but knowing it just the same, "and dangle it through the eye of the skull and where it touches the ground, *that's* where we dig for the treasure!"

Shandy handed him the telescope and nodded solemnly.

Mr. Scanlon excitedly chewed the corner of his lip. "Now why couldn't I have thought of that before? It's right there, plain as the nose on my face." He paused pensively. "In fact it seems as if I even read once about pirates hiding their treasure that way."

Shandy quickly interrupted him. "Now that we helped you figure it out, how about letting us leave?"

"You're free to go any time you like," Mr. Scanlon said. "Come on," he said brusquely to the other two men. "We've got work to do."

Shandy closed the door behind them and hurried over to untie Catfish, who was still wondering if he had heard what he thought he heard.

"Whew-wee!" Jib sagged back against a berth and stared at Shandy with open admiration. "Where did you ever dream up a story like that?"

"In school," said Shandy. "It's a story we had to read called 'The Gold Bug.' A man named Poe wrote it."

"But it fits so perfectly. You almost had me believing it."

Catfish stood up and shrugged the kinks out of his shoulders. He was still puzzled. "How come you gave up the scope so easy? That's what I can't figure."

Shandy put his finger to his lips and looked out the porthole to make sure Mr. Scanlon had left. The dinghy with all three men in it had just reached the *Raven*.

He turned back to the captain. "We don't need the scope any more," he said. "That's why I tried to get rid of them as quickly as I could. We think the treasure was moved to Crystal River."

"Crystal River!"

Shandy quickly drew a picture of what he had found on the cave wall.

Catfish studied it closely. "If it weren't for those crossed swords I'd say it was some kind of Indian picture . . . but I think you've hit it, by golly. That's the Great Spring with the good luck sign, sure as can be!"

"How soon can we get started?" asked Shandy anxiously.

"Right now," said Catfish. And he headed for the wheel-house.

They left Cockroach Bay, giving the *Raven* a wide berth as they passed, but they stayed close to the eastern shore of the big bay in case Mr. Scanlon was watching them. Once out of sight of the black cruiser, they pulled in and refueled for the last time.

Out of the marina they went at half power, skirting Passage Key. The breakers pointed to the Southwest Channel taking them across the mouth of Tampa Bay, then past Egmont Key to port and Mullet Key to starboard, northward by the rest of them—Cabbage Key, Pine Key, Long Key, Sand Key. Then Catfish was shouting, "Watch out for the Clearwater buoys!" And later it was Tarpon Springs on Anclote River and through Anclote Anchorage, then north by northwest in a dead heat across the great St. Martins Reef and into Chassahowitzka Bay with all the islands that look on the charts like the scattered pieces of a jigsaw puzzle . . . going all night . . . and by morning starting to count the keys bringing them closer: South Point, Green Key, Crawl Key and Fish Creek Bay, Long Point, Mangrove Point . . . then at last picking up the red nun buoys in Crystal Bay.

"Look sharp now, boys. Keep the reds to port and I'll take her in with South Pass to starboard, that's it. Now up the river, hi ho, pass The Rocks, Indian Mound Point, Bagley Cove where the tarpon are so thick they sound like herds of buffalo at night. Up the river, up the river, and there she is, lads, just the way we left her. Kings Bay!"

Once the *Albatross* was tied to the wharf, they headed for the Chamber of Commerce and their cigar-chewing friend, the major.

The brusque but jovial man was more than happy to see them again. And when they explained what they had come for, he was anxious to help.

"One thing's for certain," he cautioned them. "Don't breathe a word of what you're after to a soul. Mention treasure around here and you'll get run over with the competition. We've had treasure hunters roaming from one end of this county to the other with everything from converted mine detectors to divining rods. So far nobody's turned up a plugged nickel's worth of anything."

"We got reason to think it's in a cave somewhere near the spring," said Catfish.

The major took the cigar from between his teeth. "If you can find a cave deeper than a gopher hole for fifty miles around, I'd sure like to know about it. We've got some odd things in this part of Florida, but a cave would really be a tourist attraction." He chomped down again on his cigar. "Especially," he added, "since we're only four feet above sea level."

At any rate, the major promised to give them whatever assistance he could and wished them the best of luck.

When they reached the houseboat it was apparent that Catfish had made up his mind about something.

"I should have my head examined for not thinking of it before," he said. "This Indian sign that's supposed to be carved on the rock over the spring—it wasn't put there last week or last year or even fifty years ago." He thumped

Shandy's drawing with his fist. "It was put there back when maybe half this bay was dry land."

"But if the major is right and there aren't any caves anywhere around here," said Jib, "how does that tie in with the Indian sign and the spring?"

"What about an underwater cave? Maybe even the spring itself?" The captain pointed at the drawing again. "The pictures don't show a cave, just the crossed swords over the Indian sign and the spring."

"You mean maybe these pirates hid their loot when they could see this sign—when the ledge over it was on dry land?" asked Shandy.

"Could be. The spring might not always have been this big, you know. Then too, those pirate crews had scalawags from every corner of the world. It might not have been too big a job for a couple of pearl-diving savages from the South Sea Islands to handle. Why, it'd be the best hiding place in the world."

"Wow, it sure would be!" said Jib.

"I'll say," said Shandy eagerly. "Why don't we get our scuba gear ready and go look at it right now?"

"I was afraid it'd come 'round to that," said Catfish. "I don't know as I like the idea of you boys diving that far down by yourselves."

"We know how to take care of ourselves," said Shandy.

"We'll work as a team the way we always do," promised Jib.

Catfish furrowed his brow. "All right," he finally agreed. "On one condition."

"Yes, sir."

"You each gotta wear a life line down so I can haul you up if you get into trouble."

"Agreed," said Shandy quickly.

Danger
in the
Spring

STANDING on the bow of the *Albatross*, Shandy signaled Catfish to nose the houseboat a little closer to the powerful turbulence of the Great Spring. From the cabin roof, Jib shaded his eyes and studied the deep pool.

Leaning out the wheelhouse window, the captain looked past the deck winch to see how the bow was responding. He inched the throttle ahead and the houseboat shuddered as her engine labored against the strong currents.

"Ease off, Captain. We're coming into the boil too fast."

The *Albatross* slowed. "Good." Shandy scrambled back to the winch. "Hold her there a minute."

The winch squealed and the anchor chain chattered through the starboard chock. Catfish killed the engine.

The *Albatross* drifted away from the violent water, the anchor chain swung taut, and the houseboat's bow nosed back to point at the springs.

"That was easier than I thought it would be," said Shandy, making his way to the fantail where they had laid out their diving gear.

"Remember," said Catfish, "this dive is just for looking around. Don't take unnecessary chances, whatever you do."

"How would we raise a treasure chest if we did find one down there?" Jib asked as he adjusted the rubber strap on his face mask.

"Probably have to get a rope to it and run the other end around the winch to haul her up. How long an air supply have you got left?"

Shandy buckled two weighted belts around his hips. "If we take it easy we can last about half an hour. We've each got one spare, then we'll have to use the compressor on the empties."

Jib leaned over the side of the boat, spit in his face mask to keep the glass from fogging, then rinsed it out. The boys put on their rubber flippers. Catfish helped lift their heavy air tanks while they slipped their arms through the harnesses.

"Scuttle my binnacle but I wish I were going with you boys," he said longingly. "Keep a sharp lookout for rays and the like," he cautioned. "Your Aunt Tilou would skin us all alive if she knew about this."

The boys tied the safety lines around their waists. Catfish promised to pay it out to them as they needed it. "Don't try to pull us up unless we jerk on the rope twice," Shandy told him.

When everything was all set, Shandy gave Jib a nod and followed him over the side. The familiar staccato blasts of the regulator filled his ears.

He sank slowly, glimpsing shafts of blue light spangled with small, glittering fish. The boys did not try to swim, but conserved their energy so that they wouldn't waste their supply of air. The bottom came up to meet them, at first blurred and gray, then rippled tongues of snow-white sand.

Shandy touched lightly, cushioned by the water. The pressure flattened his face mask against his forehead and cheeks and there was a sharp pain in his ears. He swallowed several times to equalize the pressure and the uncomfortable feeling faded away.

He took a step and bounced like a slow-motion acrobat walking across a net. On his left were the massive brown ledges and boulders that they had seen from above. Now they were steep and foreboding, their angular faces softened by masses of seaweed that waved in the current like long green hair.

They had descended a safe distance from the main opening of the spring, but even there it was possible for Shandy to feel the strong push of the water against his body when he moved.

Out of the shadows of the tumbled boulders came the fish—bass, bluegill bream, catfish, sea trout, the brightly colored snappers. And beyond these were the bigger species watching with curiosity. A spotted jewfish with saucer-sized eyes backed into an opening between the rocks; the long silver shape of a slack-jawed tarpon hung suspended in the water, then turned and swam clamly into the blue haze. The regulators hissed and the expelled bubbles, shining like newly minted coins, scurried upward in clusters.

As they moved forward Shandy was suddenly aware of

a strong wall of pressure building up in front of them. Then the bottom dropped off abruptly and they were on the rim of a huge bowl-shaped basin that appeared to have been scooped out of the bottom. He couldn't quite make out the far side or the opening to the spring but he knew the general direction. Touching Jib's shoulder, he indicated the way with a slicing motion of his hand. Jib nodded and they started off, half swimming, half bouncing across the white sand bottom.

Partway there Shandy was struck by the immensity of the spring. What had looked small on the surface was really very large. And looking up now he saw that it was the hull of the *Albatross* that looked small, like a kite floating across a silvery sky at the end of his safety line.

A tap on his arm called his attention back to the spring. Jib pointed excitedly ahead of them. In the bluish haze Shandy saw the mouth of the spring. It was a large gaping hole with a veil of sand puffing up like smoke from its black entrance. From the surface they had not seen it because of an overhanging rock ledge, but the opening looked big enough to drive a car into. Tendrils of weed fluttered nervously on the ledge and occasionally leaves or sticks caught in the current were whipped upward by the powerful invisible force. Surrounding the basin were schools of fish— all hovering motionless and pointing toward the spring.

Moving to their left and keeping the rock wall close to them, the boys were able to approach the opening. Shandy scanned the ledge overhead, trying to locate the Indian symbol that was supposed to be there. At first he didn't see it because of the growth covering most of the rock. Then, farther to the left, he detected a crude cross carved deep in the stone. It was a foot wide and not all of the symbol was visible, but Shandy could see enough to be certain it was the same picture that had been scratched in the cave on Mound Key.

The spring itself was awesome. A geyser of water rose in front of them like a giant fountain, surging upward to make the big boil on the surface. Beyond this column was the hazy outline of the inner mouth of a cave. As Shandy leaned forward and tried to see through the curtain of agitated sand and drift, he saw the dim beginning of a tunnel. It wasn't the main one where the spring came from, but another right beside it. He was about to point it out to Jib when a shadow passed overhead and he felt a sudden surge of water against his back.

Shandy looked up just as a long gray shark curved off to avoid hitting the rock wall, turning its torpedo-shaped body into a steep bank so that only one of its broad pectoral fins grazed the tops of the weeds as it swept by.

The shark had come close enough for both boys to see its gaping mouth and five rows of sharp teeth.

Shandy made a lunge for Jib just as he started swimming for the surface. He grabbed his leg and motioned downward, shaking his head. Through his face plate he saw Jib's wide eyes, his look of terror. Shandy pulled him back to the wall, then looked back for the shark.

Suddenly he realized they were all alone. The schools of silver minnows that had reflected the sun were gone. Even the larger fish had vanished into the rocks or the dense growths of seaweed. But in the swirling blue depths that turned milky white in the distance, the shadow of the shark stood out in menacing profile as it glided back toward them.

There was no time to think. Shandy knew the wall gave them some protection but not enough. Then he remembered the double entrances at the mouth of the cave.

Half dragging, half propelling Jib beside him, he moved closer to the spring. One fear caught in his mind. If they were sucked into the uprushing torrent of water they would be as helpless as leaves in a windstorm. The shark might get them even before they reached the surface.

At the last instant Shandy glanced over his shoulder and saw the shark's ugly snout and barreled body bearing down on them. Shandy lunged through the veil of sand, dragging Jib with him.

The column of water tore savagely at his face mask and struck his body with crushing force. Then for one horrible moment he felt himself being sucked upward. He kicked, thrashing out with his flippers, pulling—and suddenly he broke through, shooting out of the torrent into the right shaft of the cave where the water was as quiet as it had been in the basin. Jib was a stroke behind him but he made it, breathing so hard that a constant stream of bubbles erupted from his exhaust valve.

Shandy nodded in relief when he saw Jib form a circle with his thumb and forefinger to show that he was all right.

The shaft of the cave they had entered was separated from the main source of the springs by a wall. Blue light filtered in through the column of rushing water outside and gave Shandy the peculiar feeling that he was sitting behind a waterfall that was going up instead of down.

Cautiously he ran his hand along the wall, feeling the chill, slimy surface crowded with sharp-shelled snails and soft-petaled marine life that shrank from his touch. Behind them was a black hole where the water moved slowly toward the entrance as it was sucked out by the spring. To take a chance of exploring it without knowing where it led and without a light was foolish. Still, they couldn't stay where they were. Shandy judged they had been down twenty minutes or more as it was. At any minute the air supply of their tanks would shut off and they would have to pull the emergency release that would give them an additional five minutes of reserve air, and that was it.

Shandy got as close as he dared to the opening of the cave and tried to see out. He could barely see the rock wall where they had crouched when they first saw the shark. Beyond that, visibility was impossible. He couldn't tell whether the shark was lurking just outside or not. In the haze their life lines looked as if they had been cut off, but he knew they hadn't.

There was nothing they could do but wait, and hope that the shark had left. Shandy heard the roar of the rushing water close by, the hiss of air exploding from the regulators after each breath. The bubbles joined and flattened themselves into a silver balloon that slithered up and fitted itself to the uneven cave roof overhead.

Jib's air was the first to shut off. When he pulled the release he held up five fingers to remind Shandy how long he had. His face was tense.

Straining to see through the haze again, Shandy found himself startled by every strange movement. A palm frond sucked into the surging currents flopped crazily upward. A black ominous shape appeared, then he relaxed as it turned into a cloud of minnows. At least their presence might indicate the shark had moved on. But how could he be certain? Abruptly his air supply ceased. He jerked the release that started the limited reserve flowing back into his lungs.

Shandy had to make a decision. In a minute or two Jib would be in trouble. If they only had something to protect themselves with . . . As the thought crossed his mind his hands felt through the loose sand on the floor of the cave. He knew they had to get to the surface quickly, and the quickest way he could think of was to let the spring blast them up as fast as it could. With luck they might get past the shark and make it to the *Albatross* before he had a chance to attack.

Shandy's hand closed on something hard and rough beneath the sand. It was heavy with sharp edges. At least it would serve as some kind of weapon.

Without worrying about the consequences, Shandy quickly signaled his plan of escape to Jib. The boy nodded that he understood.

Clutching his meager weapon in his right hand, Shandy inched his way to the mouth of the shaft. Locking hands and with a final nod, both boys pushed themselves forward into the throat of the spring.

The column of water snatched them away from the cave like a powerful magnet blasting them upward as if they had been shot from a cannon.

Seconds later they were thrashing through the boil toward the welcome sight of the *Albatross,* thirty feet away.

For some reason Catfish was standing on the roof of the cabin. Then they saw the carbine in his hands.

Halfway to the boat Shandy suddenly glimpsed a black triangular fin cutting across the surface behind him. At the same instant there was a series of loud staccato explosions that ripped the water to foam.

Catfish's powerful arms dragged them up the Jacob's ladder onto the deck, where they spit out their mouthpieces and sucked in welcome gulps of fresh air.

While they rested, the captain slipped off their equipment.

"Scuttle my keel if I ever seen the likes of that before," he exclaimed. "I thought something had got you for sure, then you shot out of those springs like demons riding a waterspout."

"What happened to the shark?"

Catfish grinned. "I stitched some buttonholes in his hide with the rifle. He never knew what hit him."

"Whew!" said Jib. "That was a close one."

"What's that you got in your hand?" asked Catfish.

Shandy was surprised to see he was still clutching the object he had picked up in the cave.

"Oh that . . . that's our shark protector," he grinned. He opened his fist and it dropped with a metallic clank on the deck.

Catfish picked it up and examined it. "Looks like a curved piece of iron." He paused. His next words came short and sharp. "By golly, it's the handle of a chest!"

*The
Sea
Monster*

CATFISH turned the handle over and over in his hands as though looking at it long enough and hard enough would tell him where the chest was.

"You say this was inside the cave and not in front of it?"

Shandy nodded. "It was right at the mouth of the tunnel."

"What kind of bottom was there?"

"Locse sand. Most of it probably drifted in from the spring. There was rock underneath."

Catfish scratched his whiskers thoughtfully. "Seems that if the pirates dropped the chest in the spring the rest of it'd be there too, doesn't it?"

The boys agreed that it did.

"You don't suppose the handle was washed into the cave by the current, do you?" said Jib.

"Not likely," said Catfish. "You fellas had a rough time

navigating that current as it was—I can't see a piece of iron doing it."

Shandy shrugged. "I don't know why we're so puzzled. The handle just broke off when they hid the chest in the cave."

"I reckon that's what we all got in the back of our minds," said Catfish slowly. "But how they worked it, and why, may be pretty important right now. Look, the cave was probably above water when the Indians put that good-luck sign on it. But if it was still dry when the pirates hid their chest, they wouldn't have been careless enough to leave evidence like this handle lying smack out in the open where anybody could see it, would they?"

"Not if they had any sense they wouldn't," said Jib.

"What about using divers?"

"That's about the only way they could have done it," said Catfish. "How long can you hold your breath, Shandy?"

"Maybe a minute or a little longer, why?"

"Some South Sea Islanders can hold theirs for five minutes," said the captain. "That'd be two and a half minutes down and two and a half coming up. If you were hauling a heavy chest to boot how far could you get it inside that cave?"

"Gosh, not very far."

"Then that's it. If we guessed right, and the chest is there, they probably didn't have time to get it very far inside. In fact, they might have been in such a hurry they didn't even have time to bother with the handle when it broke off."

It made such good sense that Shandy wished now that he had checked a few feet more of the tunnel before they had come up. The treasure chest might have been right behind him! He was anxious to get back to the cave and find out.

But Catfish wasn't too happy with the idea. "Hadn't you boys better take it easy awhile? That wasn't a picnic you just had down there, you know. What if another shark turns up?"

"We'll take Shandy's spear gun this time," said Jib. "We can leave it at the mouth of the springs where it'll be handy if we need it."

"Well, I don't—"

"We can't quit now when we're this close," said Shandy. "Something might happen and then we'd never know."

Catfish heaved a sigh. It was against his better judgment but he didn't have the heart to say no. "All right, give it a try."

The boys quickly uncoupled the empty air tanks from their diving lungs and put on the full ones. Shandy got his spear gun and an underwater flashlight out of the cabin. And he didn't forget the other important items that could mean the difference between life and death inside a cave— a waterproof compass, a wrist watch, and a depth gauge.

The captain helped them with their gear and saw to it that the safety lines were well secured around their waists. This time they decided on a new set of signals. One tug meant to let out more rope; two tugs meant to take up line; and three tugs meant they were in trouble and wanted to be hauled up in a hurry.

Then, after a quick check to make sure there were no sharks around, over the side they went.

Shandy was relieved to see that most of the fish had returned to the basin again. At the mouth of the cave the boys tugged once on their ropes for the slack they needed to get through the wall of water into the tunnel.

Shandy stuck his spear gun between a couple of rocks where he could find it easily if they needed it. Since Jib had the light, he signaled for him to go first. Jib crouched and pushed off. His flippers disappeared through the curtain of agitated sand.

Shandy counted to five slowly, then followed him. He shot out the other side like a cork popping out of a jug. Jib was waiting in the tunnel shaft with the light switched on, but it was difficult to see him through the swirling sand.

Together they slowly worked their way back into the dark cave. The roof was narrow and dome-shaped, the walls smooth. Suddenly the beam of light struck something that glittered like diamonds. Hardly daring to breathe, the boys moved toward it. The specks of light vanished and a school of frightened silvery minnows streaked past them.

The shaft went back some thirty feet before it dipped slightly then angled upward and became level. The walls of the passageway gradually became farther apart until they lost sight of the left wall entirely. The right wall turned abruptly and they followed it, flashing the light up and down the irregular surface until they came to two peculiar stone formations that thrust up from the bottom. Shandy touched one of them. Pieces of it crumbled off like chalk in his hand.

A short distance farther they thought they had found the opening to another passageway. Then they saw their safety lines coming out of it and they realized it was the one they had just left. They had gone in a circle. It was the end of the tunnel.

A feeling of sharp disappointment swept over Shandy. He had been so positive that they would find the chest just inside the tunnel that he would have bet anything on it. Now they had been over every foot of it and found nothing —nothing but a dead end.

Behind him Jib snapped his fingers to attract his attention. In the yellow glow of the light Shandy saw him examining the bottom, one that was no longer sand but mud arched up like the back of a turtle. What appeared to be bits of white shells were strewn everywhere. When Shandy reached his side Jib passed him a handful of the broken pieces and shined the light on them.

They were bones! Tiny, fragile bones.

The first thought that flashed through Shandy's mind was that they had wandered into a 'gator's den and these were the bones of his victims. But on second thought he realized they came from animals too tiny to be of interest to an alligator. In fact, they looked like bird bones.

There was only one way for birds to get into a cave, and it wasn't by swimming.

Shandy grabbed the flashlight and pointed it up. There it was, ten feet above them—an undulating silver mirror where their bubbles were not collecting in pockets as they had in the tunnel but were breaking on a surface. They both made a lunge for it.

When they shot out of water into open air the sound was deafening. Shandy lifted out the flashlight and the long yellow beam pierced the heavy blackness to reflect wetly on gleaming rock walls leaning in to form a huge dome overhead. From the ceiling hung long stone icicles exactly like the two they had found underwater in the floor of the vault.

"G-lory be!" sputtered Jib as he pushed his mask up. "We almost missed this place."

"I should have know it when we spotted those pointed rocks down below," Shandy said. "I guess what threw me off was that they only build up in a dry cave."

"Then Catfish was right." Jib looked around. "You know something else? The air in here's fresh. There must be an opening to the outside."

"Probably cracks or something," said Shandy, sweeping the light around the vault.

"Hey! What's that over there?"

"Where?"

"Over to your left . . . lower down—there!"

The full awareness of what it was momentarily stunned them. Sitting on a ledge barely out of water was a large iron chest.

With their hearts pounding too hard and too fast for either of them to speak, they wasted no time getting to the ledge and climbing out of water.

"That's *it!*" Jib whispered in awe. Look at those old padlocks."

Shandy touched the pitted, cold metal. "Gosh, it must weigh a ton! And look—a handle's missing."

They could see where it had broken from its socket. Other than that the chest looked undamaged. Hinged bars ran through iron loops along the sides. Two odd-shaped padlocks secured them at the corners.

"How'll we ever move it, Shandy?"

"Same way the pirates did." He grasped the iron handle and lifted. The chest moved heavily.

"It'll be a lot lighter in the water," he said.

"C'mon, let's get our ropes on it so Catfish can winch it out."

The boys tied half hitches around the outside of the chest and knotted the safety lines at the handle. If it broke there, the loops would still hold it.

Together they pushed it to the edge of the ledge, then shoved one end out so it was part way off the rock shelf.

"You hold the light," said Shandy. "I'll try to guide it with the rope as she goes over." He put his foot against the end of the chest.

"Ready?"

"Let 'er go!"

The chest grated against the ledge, then slipped over. Despite Shandy's effort to hang onto the rope, it was whisked out of his grasp.

A few bubbles came to the surface and that was all.

Shandy cleared his mouthpiece. "I reckon we better slide it into the tunnel, then go back and tell Catfish to hitch the ropes up to the winch."

"Yeah, we don't want anything to happen to—"

Jib never finished. The water in front of them suddenly began to heave and churn. He flashed his light across the surface. The whole pool seemed to be boiling. Then a large welt began to build up as if something huge were slowly rising up from the bottom. The boys flattened themselves against the rock wall—and then they saw it.

A hairy, wrinkled gray head as big as a watermelon rose with a gurgling hiss directly in front of them. Its tiny round eyes and mouth were almost hidden in the rolls and crevices of its hide. Its body was a giant blob more than ten feet long with two flippers in front and a wide, flat, scoop-shovel tail behind.

Suddenly Jib remembered the picture of the sea monster scratched on the scope. Sweat popped out on his forehead. His throat tightened. He wanted to cry out but he couldn't.

The creature slowly turned its wrinkled head to fasten its beady eyes on him.

At at that instant Jib dropped the light, plunging them into darkness.

New
Pirates

THE DARK VAULT echoed with the sound of thrashing water. Shandy crouched and felt along the slippery ledge until his fingers closed on the flashlight. Holding his breath, he pushed the switch. It worked. With a sigh of relief he flashed the beam across the pool.

A quick but careful look around convinced him that the thing had gone. The surface of the water was growing calm again.

He swung the beam back to the ledge. Jib was still pressed tightly against the wall, his face one shade whiter than a marshmallow.

"It's okay." Shandy tried to keep his voice from shaking. "I think he's gone now."

Jib's lips moved but nothing came out. Then a little color came into his cheeks. "W-w-what . . . was . . . *that?*"

Shandy was half guessing but he tried to sound sure of

173

himself. "I only saw a picture once but I think it was a—
a sea cow."

"A sea cow!"

"Sure, you know. They're rare animals that live in the
rivers down here. They wouldn't hurt a flea. All they eat's
weeds and things, I think."

Jib relaxed a little. "You don't sound too sure," he
said suspiciously.

"Sure I'm sure. Look, he didn't hurt us, did he?"

"He scared fire out of me!"

"Well, he did me too . . . but that was all."

"Yeah, well . . ." Jib glanced back at the pool. "For
something that eats just weeds he got an awfully hungry
look in his eye when he saw me."

Shandy shook his head hopelessly and ran a hand over
his regulator and air hose to make sure they had not been
damaged during the excitement.

He glanced at his watch. "We'd better be getting out
of here or Catfish'll be worried about us."

Jib's hands were shaking but he went through the motions
of checking over his diving gear. Finally he said, "What
about—*it*? You don't reckon it's lying in wait in that dark
tunnel, do you?"

Shandy assured him that they had probably scared the
sea cow so badly that he had kept right on going. "If it'll
make you feel any better," he added, "I'll go first."

"No . . . I was just wondering is all."

When the two of them had worked up each other's
courage enough they cautiously entered the pool, viewed its
bottom from the surface, then dove down to the chest.

They had no trouble at all sliding it across the floor of the cave to the tunnel. From there they pushed it down the sloping passageway to the incline, where they left it. Then, holding the flashlight well out in front of them, they made their way back to the mouth of the springs. Much to their relief there was no sign of the creature. They dove into the column of water and it shot them to the surface like an express elevator.

Catfish was standing by anxiously to give them a hand aboard.

"Great snakes of Medusa!" he sputtered. "If that critter didn't scare you out of your wits, I don't reckon anything ever will!"

"Then you saw him," Shandy said as he climbed over the railing.

"Saw him! I reckon I did. Biggest sea cow I ever did see. I didn't know what he'd do. Anyway, he surfaced and lit out of here in an awful big hurry. What happened?"

For the first time the boys remembered what really had happened. "We found the chest is what happened!" Jib blurted out. "It's on the end of our life lines!"

"What!"

"It's the truth. We did," said Shandy. "It's a big old iron chest and we've got it in the tunnel ready to be winched out right now!"

Catfish stared at them with his mouth open.

"Well, what are we waiting for?" he bellowed. "Let's haul it up!"

The boys scrambled aft to collect their life lines, which the captain rigged to the winch. Shandy and Jib said they

would go back to the tunnel where they could help guide
the chest.

"All right," said Catfish. "Now, if she should foul, I'll
ease off on the winch until you can free it. Two jerks on
the rope will mean she's clear, then I'll haul away. Got it?"

They nodded.

To make sure their air supply wouldn't give out on them
at a critical moment, the boys switched to the tanks Catfish
had filled with the air compressor while they were in the
cave. Then they dove back down into the springs. At the
mouth of the tunnel they followed their safety lines along
the dark passageway until the beam of their light picked
out the chest where they had left it.

From behind it, Shandy reached over and gave the rope
two hard jerks. The lines tightened and the chest slowly
slid forward.

Five minutes later it was almost to the mouth of the
cave, when the lines slackened. It was close enough now
for the boys to push it the rest of the way until finally it
sat at the very brink of the opening, ready to be lifted out.

Shandy gathered the loose ropes and jerked twice to
signal Catfish that he could winch it into the basin.

The rope remained slack.

He signaled again, thinking the captain hadn't felt the
jerks.

Still there was no response.

The boys waited a few minutes longer, then Shandy
decided he had better go up to see what was wrong.
Motioning for Jib to stay with the chest, he pushed off into
the current and started up.

Once he was clear of the springs he saw the hull of the *Albatross*. Beside it was the much larger hull of another boat. Thinking it was the major or someone else who had come over to see how they were doing, he swam for the surface.

His head barely broke water when what he saw made him duck back under again and swim hard for the cave. The boat moored beside the *Albatross* was the *Raven*!

Shandy got Jib out of the cave as quickly as he could. Then he collected his spear gun from between the rocks outside and scrawled the letters S-C-A-N-L-O-N with the tip of the spear in the sand and pointed to the boat over-head.

Jib nodded that he understood.

Shandy motioned toward shore, then wrote: GET HELP.

Jib quickly unbuckled his weight belts. Shandy handed him the spear gun and compass. Then with a wave Jib was on his way.

Shandy watched until his friend disappeared over the thick weed beds rimming the basin, then he swam back to the surface.

Mr. Scanlon was standing beside the winch with a broad grin on his face. The two gunmen were beside him. Shandy acted surprised to see them as he swam to the boat and climbed aboard.

"Hello, Shandy," said Mr. Scanlon. "I reckon you didn't expect to see us so soon after you told us that cock-and-bull story, did you?"

"No, sir," said Shandy.

"Yeah, thanks for nothin'," said one of the men. "By the time you tell anybody about this we'll be out of the country."

Mr. Scanlon whirled angrily. "Shut up, Turk!" Then instantly his manner changed. His mouth was set in a tight grin. "It took us awhile to find that hole you made on the shell island, but after that it was easy, wasn't it?"

"Hey, where's the other kid?" said Blinky.

"He's still underwater," said Shandy truthfully.

"Well now, we don't want to keep him waiting, do we?" said Mr. Scanlon. He nodded toward the ropes leading away from the winch. "Y'all just go ahead with what you were doing. We'll just watch."

Shandy looked helplessly at Catfish. The captain shook his head solemnly. "Dirty polecats got the drop on me before I could turn around," he said bitterly.

Shandy slipped off his diving lung. "Never mind," he said. "If they want it that badly we'll give it to them."

"That's the spirit," said Mr. Scanlon. "As soon as the treasure is safely aboard our boat, you can do just as you please."

"What makes you so all-fired sure the police won't have something to say about all this?" asked Catfish angrily.

"Police? What police?" said Mr. Scanlon. "We haven't broken any law—that you can prove. Now let's see about raising that treasure."

Mr. Scanlon told Catfish to start the winch again. "If either of you has any idea about trying to signal or call to shore for help, forget it," he said. "My men know how to use their guns and don't think they won't if they have to."

Catfish turned to Shandy. "Is it all right down below?"

Shandy nodded. "The chest's at the mouth of the cave. When you tighten up it'll fall into the basin. Then we can drag it across the bottom and up."

"Okay." Catfish started the winch and the slack ropes tautened. Two feet coiled tightly on the metal drum. Then the lines vibrated and fell slack again.

"It must be on the bottom now," said Shandy. "Go easy with it."

Mr. Scanlon nervously tapped his fingers on the railing. Turk and Blinky hovered over Catfish, watching every move he made. The grinding gears of the winch and the squeaking of the fenders between the cruiser and the houseboat were the only sounds to be heard.

Once Shandy glanced in the direction of the hotel, but there was no sign of Jib or anyone else on the wharf.

Slowly, foot after foot of the ropes wound on the drum. Gradually the angle between the lines and the surface of the water increased until the manila was straight down beneath them. Then the ropes quivered as the winch labored to lift the chest up from the bottom.

Mr. Scanlon paced the deck. "Easy now, easy . . . if those ropes break you'll all go over the side."

The remark stuck in Shandy's mind as the bow of the *Albatross* listed slightly. Catfish was sweating at the winch. Shandy stepped forward and offered to help. Turk pushed him against the railing and told him to stay there.

"Blinky!" barked Mr. Scruggs. "Get on that winch—we haven't all day!"

The big man grumblingly took over.

Shandy glanced hopefully toward shore again. This time there was a launch in front of the wharf and three figures were getting into it. One of them looked as if it might be Jib.

"All right, easy now," said Mr. Scanlon. "I can see the chest." He was leaning over the side and looking down into the water. Turk joined him.

"Three more turns and it'll be up," said Mr. Scanlon excitedly. "Git ready to give me a hand."

The drum turned and the last few feet of the manila rope wound onto it. The two men reached over the side and grabbed the chest. Grunting, they heaved it up to the railing and dragged it over the side of the boat.

"It must be loaded with pure gold!" Turk gasped. "Would you look at those locks!"

"There's enough here to make us rich for the rest of our lives!"

Blinky hurried to their side. "Let's blast off the lid. I wanta trickle them rubies through my fingers like sand!" he said greedily.

Mr. Scanlon grimaced. "Numskull. Start shooting out here and you'll have the sheriffs from ten counties jumping down our throats."

The noise of the approaching launch came loud to Shandy's ears but the three men were so occupied with the chest they didn't hear it.

Cautiously Shandy touched Catfish's arm and glanced

toward the oncoming boat. The captain's eyebrows twitched acknowledgment.

Shandy knew they had to do something in a hurry or there was going to be shooting. Mr. Scanlon and the other two men were sliding the chest away from the edge of the boat when he made up his mind.

With a whoop he dove straight at them.

Gray Gold
and
Something More

HE CAUGHT Turk and Blinky both off guard and off balance with a hurtling body slam that sent the gunmen head over heels over the railing into the water. Almost at the same instant Catfish leaped forward and confronted Mr. Scanlon just as he reached for the gun in his belt. He caught his arm and banged his wrist against the railing hard enough to send the weapon spiraling out into the water. Then with one hand on the scruff of his neck and the other at the seat of his pants he lifted Mr. Scanlon clear of the deck and launched him over the side right after it.

Then the captain grabbed an oar from the skiff and raised it menacingly over the three heads that bobbed, sputtering and cursing, on the surface beside the *Albatross*.

"Make one move and I'll lay this slab of pine alongside your ear so you'll be seeing stars night and day," he warned.

At that moment the launch pulled up to the stern of

the houseboat with the major, Jib, and a man standing in the bow with his gun leveled at the three in the water.

"Looks like you fellas caught a new kind of fish," grunted the major. "I can't recollect ever seein' the likes of them in the spring before."

Jib climbed out and secured the boat. He explained that the man with the gun was the hotel detective and he had called the state police before they left the dock.

"Keep your hands where I can see them," ordered the detective, "and climb aboard the houseboat one at a time."

Mr. Scanlon, Turk, and finally Blinky were hauled over the side. All three looked as if they had just crawled out of a washing machine.

The detective quickly handcuffed the two gunmen together, then told them to get into the bow of the launch. He climbed into the stern where he could keep an eye on them while Mr. Scanlon steered the boat.

"I'll take them ashore for the troopers," he said. "Thanks for wrapping them up for me."

As soon as the launch pulled away, Catfish ducked into the cabin and reappeared with a file and crowbar.

"Well," he said with a grin, "this is the moment we all been waiting for."

Everyone gathered around the chest while he went to work on the ancient locks, filing away ages of rust. With a little coaxing from the crowbar, the last two obstacles between them and the treasure broke and fell to the deck. Catfish pried back the iron bars along the side.

"All right," he said. "Shandy, Jib—this being your prize, you lift the lid."

Everyone leaned forward expectantly as the boys grasped the rough edges of the chest's lid and heaved. The rusty hinges groaned. Slowly the lid creaked open.

"Gee whiz," exclaimed Jib.

"What in blue blazes—"

"It's nothing but a big chunk of dried-up mud!" said the major.

"But it can't be!"

Catfish lifted the large, shapeless lump out of the chest onto the deck. They stared at the strange opaque gray mass.

"It sorta looks like a big piece of melted wax," said Jib.

"Maybe there's something inside it," Shandy suggested hopefully.

Catfish broke off a piece and smelled it. "It does feel like wax . . ." His eyes widened. He sniffed it again. "Why—it's ambergris!" he yelled.

"What?"

"*Ambergris*, you goggle-eyed pollywogs!" The captain started dancing around the lump like a man who had lost his senses. "About the most precious thing to come out of the sea, that's what!"

"Are you sure, Catfish?"

"Sure I'm sure," said Catfish, chortling. "Sperm whales spit it up. It's worth its weight in gold, and we got fifty pounds of it right here under our noses!"

"But how could it be worth so much?"

"Don't ask me," said the old seaman. "All I know is it's used for making perfume. Where the pirates got it is beyond me. Maybe they found it somewhere—I saw a little piece washed ashore in the Bahamas once. Maybe they stole it, who knows—who cares?"

Shandy was looking into the open chest. "That's funny," he said. "Why would an iron chest have a wooden bottom?"

"Don't know, come to think of it," said Catfish, suddenly serious again as he examined the chest more closely. "Seems it's set awfully high up for the size of it too, doesn't it?"

He picked up his crowbar and tapped the wooden bottom.

"It's hollow!" exclaimed Jib.

"Well, we'll sure see about this." Starting at one corner, Catfish worked the point of the crowbar down between the rotting wood and the side of the chest, then pried. The bottom splintered open.

They all stared in stunned silence. Emeralds, diamonds, gold crosses and chains, rubies the size of robins' eggs, pearl necklaces, gold and silver coins—all lay in a jumbled heap under the false bottom of the chest, and none of it was the less brilliant for having been buried for hundreds of years in the underwater cave.

"It's the *real* pirate treasure!" gasped Jib, holding up a small gem-studded dagger that glittered like a rainbow from the jewels that encrusted it. "We're all rich!"

"It's loot of the Spanish Main," said Catfish in awe.

"Enough to attract tourists from all over the country," said the major.

After the excitement of their find and after they had all touched the astonishing pirate plunder, someone brought up the question of what they were going to do with it for the time being.

"Safest place would be the vault at the bank," said the major.

Everybody agreed that he was right.

After all the treasure was put back in the chest and it was carried into the cabin, the major joined them on the foredeck for a last long look at the spring before they hauled up the anchor and started for shore.

"You know," he said as he looked out across Kings Bay to the distant green palm trees, "now that you fellas found what you came after I hope you won't be leaving us right away. After all, there's a lot more treasure around these parts than most people'll ever find . . . and it's all free."

"More treasure?" both boys asked at once.

"Yes sir." The major winked at Catfish. "As a starter I just happen to know where there are some 100-pound six-foot bars of silver. They're called silver kings. How'd you boys like to go tarpon fishing tomorrow?"

"Gosh, *would* we!"

"You don't reckon an old youngster like me could have a go at that treasure too, do you?"

The boys grinned at Catfish Jackson and he grinned back at them. "Yes, sir!" they chorused happily.

And so they did.

Printed in the United States
101663LV00001B/138/A

9 780595 003488